To Janet,

Rescued Retriever

enjoy —

Philip W. Comfort

Philip W Comfort

PublishAmerica
Baltim

First printing

ISBN: 1-4137-6536-X
PUBLISHED BY PUBLISHAMERICA, LLLP
www.publishamerica.com
Baltimore

Printed in the United States of America

Foreword

He was an awesome soul. Had more love in him than most folks. And more sense, too. No, I'm not talking about a saint or a godly man. I'm talking about a dog named Charlie. At one point in his life people called him Champ or Skinnie, but that was before he was rescued and loved by a girl named Heather, who named him Charlie. Heather and Charlie became more than the best of friends, they became soul mates. They learned life from each other, and they shared love.

Chapter One

Young and Eager

The sun's rays streaked through the thick green pines reaching into the tall skies as blue as the Carolina ocean a few miles away. A few blue herons stroked the air with wings as wide as angels, a sea hawk flew high overhead with a fish in its talons, cicadas hummed, and the country roads were barren except for a few racoon-faced squirrels scurrying across one patch of woods to the next. This serenity was disturbed by the motoring sounds of a pickup truck dusting its way through the gravel road on the way to the main highway. The three golden retrievers in the back of the truck barked and yelped as they rounded each curve. Bo had just taken them to the river to train them in duck hunting, and the dogs were as jazzed as could be.

Soon Bo reached Georgetown, one of the oldest cities in America—the second oldest in South Carolina. Used to be the largest port for exporting rice in the world back when there were lots of plantations and slaves working the rice fields. The Civil War changed that. But the Civil War didn't change some things. Southern boys have always loved to hunt, and they love their hunting dogs, especially labs and golden retrievers.

These "good ol' boys" are easy to spot. They drive pickup trucks with a tool chest in back, shotgun in the gun rack, Confederate flag painted on the sidewalls, with one or two hunting dogs in the flatbed barking at everything going by, or just plain barking for joy 'cause they're on their way to the river. Some call these ol' boys "rednecks." It's better to call them by their names.

Bo McCollough lived in Georgetown, as did his father and grandfather and everybody else in their lineage that his family could remember. Actually, Bo lived on the outskirts of town, in the country on a back road. His house was kind of dilapidated. The front porch slanted, the roof was cockeyed, and the whole exterior cried out for a fresh coat of paint.

Like everyone else in the area who had lived there long, Bo was accustomed to the smell of paper being processed—kind of intoxicating, like smelling Magic Markers or Elmer's glue. Some people say they miss the smell when they move away from Georgetown. But not the northern transplants in the Grand Strand. Whenever a strong southern wind comes in, they get a big whiff and say, "Whoo Georgetown, again."

Bo was about 50 years old. He had long unwashed black hair, with streaks of grey, usually tied in a pony tail, an unshaved beard, a cigarette dangling from his lips, a slight beer belly, blue jeans with rolled-up cuffs, and working boots. He worked hard during the week as a foreman in the Georgetown paper mill. His enjoyment in life was duck hunting and training golden retrievers. In fact, he made extra cash by breeding and training golden retrievers.

On weekends Bo liked to get out of Georgetown, take one or two of his dogs and go hunting. He especially enjoyed going south to the Francis Marion Woods and hanging out where Swamp Fox used to roam. The woods down there go on forever. Pines after pines, not one of them logged like other parts of South Carolina. The pines are so thick in some parts that you can't see any deeper than ten feet, to the fourth row of pines. Most of these are tall pines hanging high in the azure sky. Their crisp greenness, especially after a rain, contrasts wonderfully with the blue sky, making it ever so blue. And there are creeks running through these pines, and some hidden lakes. But mostly it is swamp. Miles and miles of swamp. A man could just go there to live, go there to die. And no one would ever know. Bo liked to go there to hunt.

On this trip, he took Sam, his four-year-old golden retriever, and he took Champ, a one-year-old. This was Champ's first time on the hunt. Bo called Champ "Skinny" because he was the runt of the last litter. "Skinny boy," Bo used to call him. Champ didn't care 'cause he could run faster than all the other dogs, and he could swim. Ever since Champ was a youngen', Bo took him to the Pee Dee River, and Champ would swim and swim. And Bo would teach him to retrieve the rubber ducks he threw into the water. It came naturally for Champ. All he had to do was hear, "Go get it, Skinny," and he dove into the river and retrieved it.

Now the time had come for Champ to learn how to retrieve real ducks. Bo's plan was to let him watch Sam retrieve for most of Saturday morning, then he would let Champ try during the late afternoon session. Bo had to leash Champ to one of the seats of the John boat during the morning session, or Champ would have jumped into the water when Sam did. Champ was anxious, so ready for the dive into the water, to swim and fetch. His body shook with anticipation. He so badly wanted to swim, but Bo wouldn't let him go in, and he would swat him on the hind end when he started to whine. That morning Champ watched Sam retrieve five ducks that Bo shot, and never once did he get to go into the water. His anxiousness turned to despondency; he thought he was being punished for something he hadn't done wrong. He curled up into a ball with his head slumped on his front paws.

Late that afternoon, Bo went out again. This time, he didn't leash Sam or Champ. Both sat in the boat, anxious, anticipating, and eager for the fetch. Champ shook with excitement but remained quiet. A flock of mallards came out from the woods on the other side of the river. There must have been 20 of them, flying in V-shape, towards their boat. Bo's heart started beating faster, as he released the safety on his shotgun, took aim, fired several times, and downed two birds. Bo then commanded, "Go get it, Sam. Go get it, Skinny." Both jumped into the water, and Champ, being more anxious than Sam and perhaps fresher, got to the first bird first. Then Sam got the other, and they both swam back to the boat with birds in mouth. Bo praised Sam.

Then he really praised Champ because this was his first time to retrieve a bird. Both retrievers shook off the river water, wagged their tails, and barked happily. Champ realized that Bo wasn't mad at him after all.

Bo shot two more birds after an hour or so, and both dogs retrieved. Champ looked like he had been doing this forever. He dove into the water flat on his belly with all his legs extended, with nose above water, snorting, and all legs kicking. With a perfect sense of direction he swam straight to the bird, opened wide his jaw, grabbed the limp mallard by the neck, turned around, and swam against the current back to Bo, who greeted Champ with high praise, then took the bird from his supple mouth, and said, "Dang, Skinny, you sure got the hang of it."

That evening Bo prepared some duck along with some potatoes he brought from home. He wrapped them in aluminum foil and put them in the coals over which he grilled the duck to perfection. He shared the feast with his dogs. They finished their meal by drinking from the cool lake water nearby; Bo finished it off by drinking a few beers.

The next day was Sunday. Bo had stopped going to church long ago. He was tired of being preached at. He was tired of never being what God, his wife, and his conscience thought he should be. But he hadn't given up on God. Bo still talked to him, especially during the night deep in the woods. And he made a point of reading his Bible on Sunday mornings. Always a psalm. He'd just open up to any old psalm and start reading out loud. This day he turned to Psalm 96, read the entire psalm, then repeated the last few verses:

Let the heavens rejoice, and let the earth be glad;
let the sea roar, and the fullness thereof.
Let the field be joyful, and all that is therein;
then shall all the trees of the wood rejoice before the Lord:
for he cometh to judge the earth;
he shall judge the world with righteousness,
and the people with his truth.

Bo liked these words, especially the idea of the trees and woods being happy. He didn't quite understand, however, what this had to do with the Lord coming to judge the earth. But he thought he was ready if that happened. He knew that his wife was ready when she died a few years back. He had learned from her.

After his Bible reading, Bo got a fire going to boil some coffee and cook some breakfast. He shared his scrambled eggs and bacon with Sam and Champ, then went out on a rather brisk November morning to begin his duck hunting. He got out just before dawn, fixed his camouflage, set out his wooden ducks, and began to make his duck calls. He hunkered down underneath his canopy of pine boughs, with his two dogs next to him, all three breathing in the brisk air. The wait was painful yet pleasant. Painful, because all three had to keep still. Pleasant, because all three were doing what they loved, and they enjoyed the thrill of anticipation. After an hour, a flock of mallards headed their way. Joe got his rifle ready, took aim, fired, and downed two, then sent his dogs after them. As usual, they dove into the water with enthusiasm, swimming and snorting and sniffing—winding their way to where the limp bodies were floating. Sam and Champ each retrieved a bird and brought it back to Bo's hands and his praise. As the day went on, Bo downed his limit of ducks, and the dogs enjoyed every fetch. Bo took his boat to shore, packed up everything, and headed back to Georgetown.

The road back is nothing but pines, with a few elms changing colors a bit in autumn. Here and there one sees a few small houses with crooked porches, and a few old churches with faded white siding and cockeyed appendage wings—built on as the congregation grew. Every church has a graveyard next to it—with lots of gray headstones shaded by angel oaks. People in those parts get baptized there, married there, and buried there. Looking at these churches, as Bo drove by, always made him pensive. He wondered about lots of things. Mostly he wondered about when he would die and what it would be like to be in one of those graves. Then he forced his mind to stop these thoughts. He turned up the country music louder and start singing along.

Chapter Two

Skinny

That week at lunch breaks at the Georgetown paper mill, Bo boasted to his friends how quickly he trained his young retriever, Champ, to fetch ducks. One of Bo's relatives, Duke, also worked at the paper mill. After downing a ham sandwich and three cartons of chocolate milk, he asked Bo, "Hey, since Champ's so good, can I take him on a weekend hunting trip?"

Not wanting to look bad in front of his coworkers, Bo said,"You can take my other dog, Sam. I think Sam's used to ya, from the other trips. But not Champ, he's a youngen'."

"Thanks, Bo. I'll come get him early Saturday."

"No, Friday. I'm headin' out Friday right quick after work."

"Okay, I'll come right soon after work and fetch Sam."

Inside his head, Bo was wrestling with this decision because he wasn't sure that Champ could do it alone. But then he determined to make the best of it. *What could go wrong, anyway?* he reasoned. *Lose a few birds?*

Bo had done all his preparation and packing on Thursday, so he was rarin' to go on Friday. At lunch, he affirmed his promise to Duke, met him at his house after work, gave him Sam, and took off south down highway 17 for the Francis Marion woods. Bo let Champ ride up front with him in the cab. Champ loved sitting high in the cab because he could check out all the scenery on the way through the pine forests. He didn't like the country music blaring from the radio—especially Bo's singing along—but Champ tolerated it because he knew they were going somewhere cool, somewhere he could run and swim.

As dusk was turning to evening, Bo set up his pop-up tent in the back of his pickup. He let Champ sleep next to him, and the two bodies kept each other warm throughout the night. Bo rose early, and as before, it was a chilly November morning—so chilly that Bo could see his breath and Champ's. Anticipating what was about to happen, Champ was eager and ready to go. Bo launched his boat into Guillard Lake, which was misty with water ascending off the smooth surface as the sun's rays began to penetrate the cold. He motored down Guillard Lake until it joined with the Santee River. He set anchor, prepared his gear, set out the wooden mallards, and began his duck calls. Bo hunkered down under the canopy of pine boughs for well over two hours until his back ached and his eyes got overstrained from looking into the sky for signs of birds. Finally, he spotted a flock of mallards, but they were too far away to shoot. Then another came, a small flock irregularly formed, with only two birds on the left of the V-shape, and fifteen on the other. As they got closer, Bo's heart beat faster. He held his breath, took aim, fired his shotgun twice, and two ducks spiraled into the river. Champ waited for Bo's command, then dove into the cool water, swimming straight to the nearest duck. He grabbed it in his mouth, retrieved it back to Bo, who took it and then told Champ, "Go get the other one, Skinny." Champ turned around in the water, kicking all four legs, glided along like an otter, came to the second bird, and realized that it was wounded, not dead. Champ hesitated, swimming around it. Bo called out, "Get it, Skinny. Bring it here!" Champ obeyed; he grabbed the duck by its neck and swam it back to the boat—all while the duck was flailing away with its wings. Bo grabbed the duck, cut off his head, and threw its body into an ice chest. Then he helped Champ back in the boat, praising him for his good work. "Good boy, Skinny! Well done!" Bo patted him on his head, rubbed his ears for awhile, and then lit up a cigar to celebrate the occasion. "We did it, boy! We did it! Gonna have some good eaten' tonight."

Champ sat there all proud. He knew he had passed the test. He knew that he had done what he was born to do and he loved it. He wagged his tail, sat next to Bo, and lifted his right paw up for Bo to shake. Bo shook it, like man to man, and said, "Lord, we did good, Skinny." And then the rains came. Lots of it. So Bo and Champ went back to the Guillard Lake campsite and got into the cab of the truck to wait out the rains. Bo started the engine, turned up the heat, then turned on the country music again. Champ tried to sleep, but it was hard to do with the music blasting.

After they got warm and the rains stopped, Bo started to prepare the birds for supper. "Not gonna take these home. We're gonna eat 'em up tonight." As Bo went around to the back of the truck to get some cooking utensils, Champ started barking.

"What is it, boy?" Hearing some leaves rustling nearby, Bo dropped the utensils, grabbed his shotgun, and swung around to where he heard the noise.

A voice called out from behind a group of pines, "Ya'll makin' such a racket, I had to see what was goin' down. Ya can put the shotgun down. Might kill somebody."

Champ kept barking till Bo told him to hush. Then he asked the man, "Are you a duck hunter?"

"You said it."

"Where ya camped?" Bo asked.

"Down yonder. Wanted to do some more huntin', but lost my dog."

"How?" Bo asked, now relaxing a bit.

"He ran off on me today. How's your retriever?"

"He's right good."

"Youngen', ain't he?"

"Yea, but right good."

"You don't suppose I could hunt with ya tomorrow? I'll give ya all I catch."

"We'll see," Bo replied. "Come first thing in the morning."

Bo couldn't make out his face real clearly in the darkness. But he looked to be about 40, had a beard, long hair tied in a ponytail, hunter's clothes, and carried a walking stick. Bo repeated himself, "We'll see in the morning," then returned to his utensils to start preparing the birds for supper.

"Thanks," the man answered. "My name's Jackson. Folks call me Jack."

"I'm Bo. See ya tomorrow."

After the man left, Bo cooked dinner, shared some charcoal duck with Champ, and then bedded down for the night in his pop-up tent on the back of his truck. Champ crawled in and slept next to him. At first morning light, Jack was there waiting for them. He had brought some freshly made coffee and some donuts.

"Mornin', Bo. Hoped you slept well. Have some coffee and some Dunkin Donuts. Only two days old."

They both laughed. Bo, thinking he'd enjoy the company, invited Jack to hunt. "Com' on, we'll share the dog. He'll retrieve for both of us."

Both men were experienced duck hunters, so they exchanged the common lingo as they set off to what they thought was the best site on the Peedee River near Guillard Lake. They prepared the camouflage, set out the wooden mallards, and started making duck calls. After awhile, a flock of mallards headed their way. They both rose to their feet, took aim, and fired their rounds. Three ducks fell, and Champ, jumping into the river, immediately got to work. For him, it was natural joy, swimming along at a fast clip, snorting in the crisp air, fetching one duck after the other, and bringing them back to the men, both of whom praised him: "Good boy, Skinny. Good boy!"

Another flock and another round of fire brought them another three birds, each retrieved by Champ. As the November sun made its highest arch into the cold blue sky, the two men decided to head back in, make some lunch, and then go out again at dusk. As they were bringing the boat down the river, Bo spotted a flock of wild turkeys a hundred yards away, wandering through the woods. So did Jack. They quickly pulled the boat up to shore, grabbed their guns and amo, and started to stalk the turkeys. In an instant, Bo caught sight of the turkeys, ran up a little hill, and began firing. Jack, at a different angle, also began firing. The turkeys ran behind a cluster of swamp magnolia, and then headed away from the river. Bo reloaded and took off after the turkeys. Jack did the same, coming right behind Bo.

Both men began running, hearts throbbing, adrenaline pumping, enjoying the hunt. As he ran down a small embankment, Jack's foot hit an exposed root of a live oak, causing him to trip, fall, and accidentally fire his gun when he landed on the ground. The blast went straight into the back of Bo, who screamed, fell flat, and went into immediate cardiac arrest. Jack got up, went to Bo, turned him over, and began CPR. But it was no use. Soon his pulse stopped, his breathing ceased, and Bo's spirit left his body.

At first, Jack just stood there, dumbfounded. He couldn't believe what just happened. He tried CPR for another minute or two, then gave up. He started to leave the site, then he turned back around, grabbed Bo's body, and dragged him by the feet to the boat. Jack placed Bo's body in the boat, covered it with pine boughs, then shoved the boat off into the river. He stood there for a moment watching the boat slide southward in the current, then he ran back to his own campsite, gathered up everything, cleaned up everything, and drove away.

Chapter Three

Out on His Own

At the moment Bo's spirit left this world, Champ took off deep into the woods, frightened and uncertain. He returned to the campsite late that night, climbed up into the pop-up tent in the flatbed of Bo's truck, and fell asleep. In the morning, he nosed his way into Bo's backpack and grabbed all the food in there—six packets of Slim Jims (Bo's favorite), two packs of black licorice, and a small box of dry dog food. Champ took these, in turn, to an oak tree hundreds of yards away from the campsite, where he worked on ripping open a packet of Slim Jims. After eating a packet, he wandered over to where Bo had been killed, smelled around the whole area, rolled in the dirt mingled with Bo's blood, peed on the trees nearby, and then went back to the campsite.

As the sun rose higher in the sky, the day got warmer, unusually warm for November. Champ went to the lake for a swim and a long drink. He spent the day going from the campsite to the death-scene to the river, trying as best he could to put the whole thing together in his mind. He kept expecting Bo to show up. But he didn't. Not that day, which was Monday, or the next day.

When Bo didn't show up for work on Monday, no one thought anything of it. They figured he was probably sick or still hunting or something. But when he didn't show up to work on Tuesday, Duke got a bit concerned. "It's not like Bo. He'd call in," Duke told their boss. Duke was sure that something was wrong because he thought

Bo told him to bring his dog, Sam, back on Monday. Since there was no sign of Bo at the house, Duke called the police and told them where they might be able to find Bo. The sheriff's office sent out a sergeant, who then took Duke with him to look for Bo.

Duke had been to Bo's favorite spot near Guillard Lake once or twice, so he was fairly sure he'd know just where to go. Speeding down highway 17 at well over 75 miles an hour and then on to country road 45 and down several other narrow country roads, they got there before sunset, saw Bo's truck, and started to examine the scene. Both men kept calling out, "Hey, Bo! Are you there?" But there was no answer.

The sergeant began to explore the area around the campsite. As he started down the trail weaving through pines that led to the river, he saw a golden retriever coming up the hill. "Hey, Duke. Is this Bo's dog?"

Duke came over to the trail, and Champ came up to Duke rather tentatively. Duke held out his hand and said, "It's okay, Champ. Good boy." Then he pet Champ for awhile to calm him down. "Where's Bo? Take us to Bo."

Knowing what he was asking, Champ barked, then briskly walked into the pinewoods toward the scene of the shooting. When he got there, he wimpered, pawed the ground, and peed on the tree nearby. The sergeant and Duke bent down, and could see that there had been blood spilled there. Then Champ headed down a trail to the river, and they followed. When he arrived at the river's edge, he started barking and spinning in circles.

Duke got the point right away. "He's telling us that Bo was hurt and then went off in his boat." Duke then directed a challenge to Champ: "Where's Bo? Where's Bo?" Champ jumped in the river and started paddling downstream and kept going until he was clean out of sight. The men followed along the riverbank for awhile, but couldn't go any farther because there was a swampy, mucky inlet that impeded their progress. So the men trudged back to the patrol car to plan their next step, while Champ kept paddling downstream until well after sunset. He got out of the river about five miles downstream, having never found Bo or his boat. Exhausted and shivering, he found an indentation between two pines, and curled up to sleep in a bed of pine straw.

As the wind moaned, owls hooted, and red fox wandered the woods in search of mice, Champ slept as best he could, even though he kept shivering. In the morning he headed back to camp, walking upstream along the river trail the entire way. The sun broke through the clouds in the eastern sky and streamed through the woods, spotlighting here and there with its golden rays. Along the way, Charlie would pause in these spots, to bathe in the sunlight, which so warmed his body and soul. Then he kept going, walking on trails of mud and pine straw, weaving his way through tall pines and a few live oaks. Eventually, he located Bo's truck, jumped into the back cab, and dragged Bo's sleeping bag far into the woods, placing it next to the live oak where he had kept the food. He then ripped open one bag of Slim Jims and then another and then another. He devoured them with relish, then settled down for a warm nap in Bo's sleeping bag, after which he went down to the river again. Yet one more time, Champ was determined to swim after Bo and find him.

As Champ was swimming the river, the police came to inspect the campsite and surrounding area. They took pictures of the area, especially the scene of bloodshed, and then towed away Bo's truck. When Champ got back to the campsite late that evening, there was no more truck and no more tent. He found the oak where he had placed Bo's sleeping bag, ate the last of the Slim Jims, and went to sleep.

For the next four days, Champ repeated his routine of swimming the lake and river during the day in search of Bo, then returning late in the afternoon to the campsite. He had finished the black licorice and the small box of dry dog food. There was no more food. On the fifth day, he left the area and headed southeast on Guillard Lake Road toward highway 45. As he walking along, the sound of men shouting and shotgun blasts scared him. Champ quickly turned around and headed back to the river, following the river trail southward.

He went three days without anything substantial to eat, nibbling only here and there on some grass. Then farther down the trail under a fallen oak he smelled a burrow of moles. He dug and dug until he reached one of the moles, grabbed it by the tail with his teeth, shook it, then killed it. Having never eaten any animal uncooked before, Champ was reluctant to bite down. So he sat there for about an hour examining his prey. Then, driven by hunger, he took a bite and then another until he finished it off.

Unknown to Champ, the smell of fresh blood attracted a few wild boars, which quickly and stealthily encircled Champ. Boars, like wolves, hunt in packs. He held them off as long as he could by barking, growling, and showing his fangs. He spun in circles and kept growling with as much velocity as he could vigor. But the boars kept closing in on him. The largest boar lowered its head, charged Champ, caught him on the underside with its tusks, and flipped him over its head outside the circle of boars. Luckily, Champ landed on his feet and took off running toward the river, with the boars in full pursuit. Champ dove in and started paddling at full tilt. The boars didn't pursue.

Champ crossed the water to a small pea-shaped island in the middle of the river. He got out, shook and shook, then tended to his bleeding wounds by licking his stomach over and over. Champ moaned and moaned, drank from the river, and tried to sleep.

Chapter Four

Caught

Alone on the island, Champ's only companions were pain and misery for nearly a week. Fortunately, the wounds on his stomach were starting to heal because Champ licked these wounds over and over. God must have put some healing juices in saliva. After all, Jesus healed people with spit. And that's the first thing people do when they cut a finger—they put it into their mouth. Spit heals.

But Champ had eaten nothing for almost ten days. He lived on nothing but God, some sunlight, air, and especially water. Somehow he knew that he had to drink a lot of water to compensate for his loss of blood. He drank and drank, but he was getting thinner and thinner. Already skinny, his ribs were showing more than ever beneath his muddy golden coat. His brown eyes had lost their luster and glow. To add to his misery, he had ticks all over him, especially behind his ears. There were ticks upon ticks. He spent hour after hour using his hind legs to scratch behind his ears. But the ticks were winning.

If humans could read dog's minds, they would hear Champ thinking, *how I'd love to dissolve into this air, this streak of sun, to live on something other than water. Or to slip into the next life—to swim freely in warm water and air.* Some will say that's putting into a dog's mind what humans think. Really? Doesn't all creation seek freedom for their souls and bodies? Anyway, Champ wasn't thinking good thoughts. But he hung in there anyway, hoping to see Bo again, hoping to feel well again. "Hope springs eternal," the poet says. And maybe he's speaking for every living creature.

The days were getting shorter; the sun thinner and air crisper. The winter sun was making its arch far too quickly. Champ spent most of his days following its movement to get the maximum amount of heat. He didn't like late afternoons because that meant the sun would be leaving him. Late one afternoon, just before dusk he heard a duck hunter blowing his whistle across the river and then he heard shotgun blasts. Charlie stood up, perked his ears, and cocked his head, straining to listen more closely. But when the hunter called to his dog, he could tell it wasn't Bo's voice. Still, Champ thought he might join them, but he felt he didn't have the strength to make the swim. He tried barking to get their attention, but that didn't work. His bark was too feeble. In the distance, he saw a dog fetch a bird, take it to the boat, and get into the boat, which then sped away into the dusk melting into darkness.

Another night passed of Champ hearing owls hoot, coyote croon, and wild boars snort against the fall of darkness. Another day of earth rising and Champ rising to the challenges at hand. He drank some water, peed on a pine tree, then entered the river to make the long swim. The current was heading southward. So every yard he made eastward he also went a yard southward. He paced himself, kicking his back legs with even strokes, paddling with his front paws with intermittent bursts of energy. With nose above water, he snorted and sucked, using every muscle in his weak body to make it to the other side alive.

Exhausted beyond belief, he made the last kicks to the mucky shore on the other side. Unable to move each paw freely in the sinking mud, he stood there for awhile on all fours gasping for breath. Then, paw by paw, he inched his way out of the mud to the sandy clay on the brink of the riverside, where he lay down.

Champ slept for a whole day. He didn't go to paradise or dog heaven. He just got a real good rest. Revived, he took a long drink of water, lapping up as much river as his stomach could take. Then he went around lifting his leg on tree after tree, leaving his talisman here and there. He made his way back to the campsite, sniffed everything, found three Slim Jims covered with ants, and ate all three. Then he headed out, trying to find his way back home to Georgetown.

Champ wandered down Guillard Lake Road, a thin strip of gravel lined with pine tress. He came to highway 45 and turned north. A few cars came speeding by, one nearly hitting him. He ran into the woods and eventually came to a thin gravel road known in those parts as 271 heading southeast. This road was completely unpopulated except for a few turkey vultures gnawing on the last bits of a dead rabbit. He then headed south on a narrow gravel road known as 160, then southeast again on what's called Hell Hole Road, which is a narrow one lane road snaking through ten square miles of swamp water, cypresses, gators, snakes, and muck.

On the first day he wandered through this swamp searching to catch anything to eat. He caught nothing. On the second day he discovered moles burrowing under a fallen cypress. The scent of live prey spurned him on—past his strength—to keep digging. His front claws grabbed the mucky dirt, thrusting it back through his spread-out back legs. He kept doing this until there was a mound behind him and a hole in front of him. Then he would stick his snout into the hole to smell for the moles. One of the moles, now exposed, tried to make a run for it. But Champ grabbed it by the neck, immediately killing it. This time, Champ didn't dally. He started consuming his catch immediately.

Champ moved on, past Hellhole Swamp to the Big Opening. In this part of the swamp there is nothin' but muck, broken cypress trees, an occasional egret, blue heron, and racoon-faced squirrel. From there he wandered into another swamp area known as Darlington Swamp. Late in the afternoon he was heading southeast toward Thomas Corner when he heard some human voices. Champ cocked his head and perked his ears to get a better listen. He heard men's voices and dogs barking, so he moved closer but didn't let himself be seen. Truth was, he was leery of human beings, after what happened to Bo. But the smell of food cooking lured him.

Soon he found himself in the backyard of a broken-down hunting cabin taking handouts of hot grilled duck from the hands of a redneck named Ret. Slim ate several mouthfuls of the best eatin' he had in weeks, wanted more, but then Ret grabbed him, collared him, and put him in a dog run with another golden retriever named Babe. Champ looked at Babe for awhile, sniffed her, and then consumed the rest of her dry dog food in a filthy dirty bowl. He then lapped up all the water in a bucket nearby. Babe didn't seem to mind.

Ret went inside and told his hunting buddy named Ben, "Got us another huntin' dog. Just walked up out o' nowhere."

Ben responded, "What luck! We'll try him tomorrow."

The next morning came, sunless, damp, and cold. The two men took their dogs to Gulliard Lake and on to the Santee River near the spot Bo used to hunt. They set out their boat, decoys, and prepared their gear. They leashed Babe and Champ to the seats of their fishing boat. While the men waited, they smoked, cussed, and told dirty jokes. Champ didn't like their company at all. Eventually, a small flock of mallards headed their way. The whir of wings and duck-honks announced their arrival. Ret and Ben sprung into action. They shot two mallards, then unleashed Babe and Champ to go fetch them. Without hesitation, both dogs leaped into the cold water and swam straight to the dead ducks. When Champ returned with his first fetch, he was praised. Ret turned to Ben and said, "Look's like we'ze got us a trained dog!"

"Yea. At someone else's sweat and nickel!"

They shot down a few more mallards that morning, fetched by Babe and Champ, then went back to the hunting cabin for lunch and a nap. Champ rested in the dog pen, ate more dry dog food, drank the rainwater in the bucket, found the corner where there was some sunlight, and slept until he and Babe were aroused by Ret and Ben who had decided to go quail and turkey hunting. "Let's try the new dog on quail or turkeys," Ret said.

"Sure," Ben agreed, taking another bite of Redman's and spittin' on the ground. Ret leashed Champ, and Ben leashed Babe. Then they went to an open area south of Hellhole Swamp and started traipsing though the tall swamp grass. Soon Babe picked up a scent of live bird. She immediately went into a point. Her face stiffened, her nose pointed southward, her front right leg lifted, and her tail straightened—as she stood still as a tree. At Ret's command, she flushed out the quail who ran then flew, only to be downed by shotgun blasts. The two dogs ran after the birds, each retrieving one.

After another hour of walking, Babe got wind of other birds. She stopped and pointed. But Champ ran after the birds, scaring them and dispersing them into the woods. Ret went after Champ, grabbed him, and started beating him mercilessly—smashing him across the muzzle with the back of his hand. Champ whelped in pain and cowered in the grass, as he got beat up bad. Ben watched for awhile and then said, "Guess you done got only a duck dog there, man."

"Shut up," Ret retorted, as he leashed Champ, and drug him behind, nearly gagging him to death.

As the day was coming to an end, a thin swath of sunlight spread across the western horizon. Like a sleepy eye it would soon shut and night would begin. Ret and Ben were about to turn back toward home, when Babe caught scent of birds and started to point. At Ben's command, Babe flushed out the quails. A whir of fluttering wings and bird-scare grunts revealed two bodies emerging from the tall grass and ascending. The shotgun blasts rocked the air, and two twirling torsos descended with separate thuds. The two dogs took after the birds. Babe got to his first, grabbed it and turned back. Champ reached his bird, hesitated, then took off running away from the men. By the time they realized that Champ wasn't going to return, he had put nearly 100 yards between them. He kept running deeper into the swamp, not about to look back.

Chapter Five

Found

Once Champ got away from his captors, he could think clearly. In his mind, he told himself not to get near humans, especially those that looked like hunters. This became fixed in his psyche. He spent yet another evening in Hellhole Swamp—cold, shivering, with a bloody mouth, and abandoned. Yet he'd rather be alone than with humans.

In the morning he made his way back to the Pee Dee River, took a long drink of the cool water, and soaked in the bright winter sunlight beaming through the leafless trees. He got his belly full of water and his thin body warmed by the sun. He was hungry, but didn't have the energy to hunt. He spent most of the day resting and licking his wounds on his mouth. Ret had hit him so hard across the muzzle that his teeth had punctured his gums.

The next day Champ searched for burrows, found one, and dug like a madman until he exposed a mole, which he caught and consumed. As he was eating the last part, he heard human voices not too far away. So he took off toward the river, dove in, and swam to the other side to a place known as Santee Swamp. Champ made this his home for the next weeks. As November passed into December, the cold got colder, the wind got fiercer, and the food got scarcer. Without knowing it, Champ was dying of pneumonia and malnutrition.

He couldn't get enough air into his lungs to make the swim back to the other side. Day after day he wandered southeastward and finally found himself opposite McConnel's Boat Landing. Some boaters spotted him, crossed the river to get him, and took him into their boat. The two men could tell he was nearly dead, as he lay in the bottom of the boat shivering and weezing. When they crossed back to the other side, they thought they should take him to a vet somewhere. They docked, tied up their small boat at the landing, and headed for their truck and trailer with the intention of hauling in their boat and heading into McLellanville to find help for the dog. But when they got back to the boat, Champ was gone and nowhere to be seen.

For the next three days Champ wandered eastward through the Wambaw Creek wilderness. He spent another lonely night in the graveyard of St. Peter's church, hunkered behind the gravestone of some long dead soul to keep him out of the direct wind. He spent another bitter night in the Little Wambaw Swamp, burrowing himself into pine straw to keep himself as warm as possible during an evening of cold rain. The next day he forced himself to keep moving. He skirted Buck Hall, and neared Highway 17 to the south. The longer he walked, the thirstier he got, with no sign of water anywhere. For a few moments, he thought he should turn back to the river, but then the sound of automobiles and trucks motivated him to keep going toward the highway.

When he reached the berm, car after car sped by, even truck after truck—many hauling tall pine logs. Champ stood there frozen, a pathetic figure, hardly looking like the golden retriever he really was. He stood there numb, not knowing what to do next. Cross to the other side? For what? Stay put? Keep going on? Where? He walked along the berm, heading north against the traffic, logging trucks whizzing by him at 60 miles an hour.

After walking for fifteen minutes, a car pulled up alongside him. The woman in the car leaned over, opened the passenger door, and called to him, "Come on. Come on in." Champ didn't have the energy to climb into the car, so the woman got out, walked around, and hoisted him into the passenger seat. The two looked at each other in the afternoon sunlight. She saw his sad brown eyes, and he saw her charitable blue eyes. "Somehow I know you," she said. His eyes said the same.

Realizing how thirsty he looked, she took a McDonald's cup from off the floor and poured her bottle of purified water into it. She placed it before his mouth, and watched him lap up as much he could get. She had to tip the cup so that his tongue could get more. Then she had to rip off the top section of the cup all the way around so he could get his tongue to the bottom of the water. He drank and drank until there was nothing left. She then poured out the rest of another bottle of water she had in the back seat. And he drank all of it and burped.

The woman then put her car in gear and drove down highway 17 past Pineland and Awendaw, then into Mt. Pleasant, where she found a veterinarian hospital and asked them to take care of the dog. They declined but recommended another vet down the road, who welcomed this scroungy half-dead dog. The vets at this clinic gave Champ a flea and tick bath, an IV solution of fluids and nutrients, and a few dog biscuits. The vets extracted over a 100 ticks, applied some antibiotic cream to his stomach and jaw, and thoroughly bathed him.

When the woman, named Jenny Thomson, returned hours later to get him, they brought a dog out from the back room fully groomed. "Here's your dog," the veterinary assistant said with a smile.

"No way!" Jenny said. "She's a beautiful golden retriever! I thought it was a mut or something."

"Not a she, ma'am. He's a he."

As the two women were laughing and gloating over this newly found, newborn creature, the vet, Dr. Carmichael, came out, shook Jenny's hand, and thanked her for rescuing this wonderful animal. With a deep Southern draw, he said, "Wish there were more folks like you, ma'am. You did well to rescue him. There'll be no fee for our services. Just find him a good home—ya hear. He needs lots of water. Lots of rest. Some food eventually, when his stomach can take it. And he needs lots of love."

"Oh, we'll give him all that and more," Jenny beamed. "Thank you so much for your help, sir." Jenny then bought the dog a matching collar and leash, put them on him, and marveled at how good he looked. But as she started leading him to the car, Champ bit at the leash, and balked against getting in the car.

"What's the matter, boy? I'm not gonna hurt ya."

After being gently coaxed, Champ reluctantly got in the car, and Jenny drove down to Charleston, where she was going to meet her husband, Paul, to watch their daughter, Heather, play a high school soccer game.

Chapter Six

A Yankee and a Retriever

Heather was a newcomer from the North. As a Yankee, she had hardly made any friends when she moved to South Carolina from Columbus, Ohio. But she was an extremely good soccer player, even at the age of 14, so the coach gave her a starting position as center forward on the girl's varsity soccer team. At first, this helped her make a few friends, even though they were older. But as the soccer season went on and she became the leading scorer, the jealousies grew and she was ostracized.

This particular game was an important one; it was for the regional championship. Heather had already scored two goals in the first ten minutes. She was congratulated by her teammates for the first goal, but not the second. As she walked back to the center of the field for the next kickoff, Heather told herself, "No more goals. Just passes and assists."

Paul was watching his daughter's soccer match, when his wife came walking into the stadium with a dog moving slowly next to her. She brought him up into the stands, and told the soccer parents sitting around her the story about how she found him. *Just like my wife*, Paul thought. *She has a knack for picking up strays.*

Then Paul told Jenny, "Hey, Heather has scored two goals already. She blasted one into the upper corner, and the other was a volley off a rebound."

"Great!" Jenny responded, who then told some of the parents sitting there, "Paul will think I'm crazy if I ask him to keep this dog.

We already have two other dogs at home."

Overhearing her, Paul said, "No, I've always wanted a dog like this." Then Paul pet the dog's back. "You're really thin. We'll put some meat on ya, boy."

The other team, the Charleston Kicks, tied up the game by halftime. Heather had two other opportunities to score, but each time she passed to another player who missed the shot on goal. At halftime, the coach told her to keep shooting and told her teammates to keep getting the ball to her. But Heather persisted in the second half with her plan. She would not shoot; rather, she looked for the closest player and passed. Fifteen minutes into the game, Charleston scored again, giving them a three to two lead. Heather's coach substituted her and talked to her point blank, face to face, "I see what you're doing. But varsity soccer is not about making friends. Get in there and shoot when you can."

Heather went back into the game. Within five minutes she tied the score. This time all her teammates gave her high-fives. With two minutes left to go in the game, Heather got a pass in the corner of the penalty box, then she distributed the ball straight down the 18-yard line to her teammate, a halfback, who cocked back and kicked the game winner into the opponent's net. There were cheers all around, and everyone was cool with Heather.

After the soccer match, Jenny and Heather rode home together from Charleston to Pawleys Island. Jenny congratulated her on her game, then told Heather the story of how she found the dog: "I was driving along, thought I saw a baby deer along the road as I went by, and feared it would get hit by a logging truck. So I made a U-turn, drove up to the animal on the berm and discovered it was a dog, not a deer." Then she related how well the vets took care of him, saying, "The vet thinks he must have been in that woods for more than a month. Suffered a wild boar attack, lost lots of blood, has a slight case of pneumonia, and got quite emaciated."

"I'm so glad he was rescued. Let's keep him, Mom," Heather said. "He's so cute."

"Yea, that's what Dad thinks, too."

"What'll we call him?" Heather queried.

"How 'bout Charleston?" Jenny posed. "Since we found him near Charleston."

"That's cool," Heather said, as she looked into the back seat and saw him curled up asleep.

Jenny and Heather took Charleston to his new home in Pawleys Island, a home set in the pine woods about two miles from the ocean. During the first weeks in his new home, Charleston regained his strength, soaking in all the love he could get. When he approached Paul, Jenny, or Heather he would sit before them on his two back legs, and lift up his front right paw for them to shake. He did this for a few minutes, then he would lay down to sleep. Then he would get up after an hour or so, find the nearest person, sit in front of them on his back legs, and lift up his front right paw for them to shake. Whenever he did this, he panted a bit—opening his mouth slightly, exposing his moist pink tongue and a few white teeth. Too adorable. His chiseled jaw, his protruding chest with a swirl of golden hair, and whole demeanor glowed. Then he would wane, go back to the corner of the living room, find the winter sunlight wherever it was coming in, and lay down for a nap.

This went on for several weeks, while Charleston regained his strength. His first outing with the family was to the beach. When they got there, Charleston jumped out of the car and started running up and down the beach. It was his first time to the ocean, and it showed. He chased every sandpiper, every seagull, even every pelican. But all were too fast for him. And they could fly. But he kept chasing them anyway until he ran out of energy.

There on that December day, full of sun and brisk wind whirling from the north down the beach, Heather fell in love with Charleston. She loved how he ran, how he sat, how he glowed with life. He brimmed over, more than the ocean. He was effulgent with joy—just the joy of being alive. He came up to Heather, sat in front of her and extended to her his front right paw. She took it, shook it, then got down on her knees to embrace Charleston. Taking a deep whiff of his rich verve, of his canine aliveness, she connected with his soul. It startled her at first, having never connected with an animal's soul before, but then she enjoyed it. Charleston was a "person," not a human person, but a person nonetheless, and Heather sensed it. And Charlie knew.

"Oh, Charlie," she said, "I'm so glad we found you."

His deep brown eyes said the same.

Chapter Seven

Dog Lovers

The Thomsons were dog lovers, so Charlie was not the only dog in their household. There were two others, named Nanook, a Siberian husky, and Rudy, a German shepherd. And just before Charlie, there had been another named Barney, a Shetland sheep dog. Barnie was no longer with the Thomsons when Charlie arrived. He had already gone on to dog heaven. And Nanook, quite sadly, would soon pass on. Nanook hardly knew that Charlie had come into the household. It was a different story with Rudy, which we will get to after the lives and adventures of Barnie and Nanook.

Barnie was a wonderful creature. He had a habit of circling everything and everyone. He could run in circles for hours, herding children, geese, and ghosts. He barked and barked, which drove most people crazy. (The neighbors loved him!) But he was sweet. He loved the children as they were growing up in Columbus, and they loved him. He excelled as a backyard soccer player, especially at defense. He took many a shot into the ribs and head for the sake of the team. He chased the geese in the nearby ponds and felt so proud that he made them all fly away. And he was quite adept at chasing down sledders as they sped down the snowy hills in winter. Barney knocked many a kid over—sort of linebacker style. This aspect of Barney's talents would always surprise people; it sure surprised the little kids coming down on the sleds. And I must also mention that Barney wasn't patriotic; he hated the Fourth of July. The fireworks freaked him out. Most of all he liked his ears scratched, and he loved steak bones—what dog doesn't?

A few years after Barnie lived with the Thomsons, he got a companion, Nanook. He was Mom's gift to her son, James, who wanted so badly to have a Siberian husky. Nanook was sleek, silver-white, with piercing blue eyes. It was hard to stare at him without thinking how powerful his soul was. He was an awesome creature of God.

But Barney and Nanook did not jive. In fact, it took several years before they would. Nanook was strong, aggressive, and dominating. The Alpha dog took over, and Barnie surrendered to his lordship. Once this was established, Nanook got to the business at hand, which was to run and run and run and run, and then run and run and run. He wore out the dog run. He'd nearly pulled James' arm out of his socket when he took him on walks—or should I say "runs." So James gave up the traditional method of walking the dog. Instead, he grabbed his leash and let Nanook pull him around on his roller blades. In the winter, James hooked him up to a sled so he could pull kids around. All Nanook wanted to do was run and pull.

Every chance he got, when the front door was opened just a bit, Nanook would dash out the door and run for hours all around the neighborhood. Dr. Thomson built the fence higher and higher in the backyard, but he'd find ways to jump it. When James first got his driver's license, he spent many an evening driving around the neighborhood looking for Nanook. Usually, he'd find him miles away, playing with some other dogs or raiding someone's garbage cans.

One winter evening James returned home distraught. He hadn't found Nanook. And Nanook stayed away the whole next day and night. The following morning James and his dad drove to the dog kennels, hoping that one of the dogs there was Nanook. But it wasn't. On the way home, his dad told James, "Well, son, we can get another dog some day."

"But, Dad, I've been praying for him. I want Nanook," James said mournfully.

Instead of taking the normal route from the kennels to Dr. Thomson's place of work, where James would drop him off and then head on to school, Dr. Thomson saw a back road he thought would get them there quicker. "Turn here," he told James. Not more than 100 yards down this side road, Dr. Thomson yelled out, "Look, it's Nanook!"

James got out of the car, and pulled him away from rough-housing with another dog. Nanook was wet with dirty snow and panting. As they drove on to work, which was five miles from their house, father turned to son and said, "There is a God after all!"

James went to college a few years later, and he took Nanook with him for his sophomore year at Ohio State. Barnie stayed with the family for several more years, making the move from Columbus to South Carolina. He spent his last months in South Carolina, walking the beach, enjoying the company of Nanook, who also enjoyed his final days in the Deep South—though it was way too hot for him in the summer. Both Barnie and Nanook strolled the beach together, looking for food, looking for shade, sloshing through the shallow waters. Sadly, both Barnie and Nanook passed on within a short time of each other—one then the other going into dog paradise, where there are endless trees to pee on, bones galore, soccer balls, and lots of other dogs.

Though bereft of Barnie and Nanook, the Thomsons weren't left without a dog. They had a wild one, a German shepherd named Ruddy. One of those gifts-from-the-oldest-son-who-couldn't-keep-him-in-the-apartment. You know. Now Rudy was smart, inquisitive, and mean. Nothing got by Rudy. At any sound, he would cock his head, tilt his ears, and listen. He would really try hard to understand anything anyone said. And often he did. He knew the words "num-num," "beach," "car," "door," "bone," "stick," and "get it."

He loved to have a job. So the family gave him one—that of guarding the house. No one got in if he didn't want them in. After a long hot day of guarding the house, Rudy loved to go to the beach in the evenings—so much so that he barked the whole way there incessantly. The more the Thomsons told him to shut up, the more he barked. It was insane. They tried to muzzle him, spray him, even put him in the trunk. He freaked out. Went ballistic. Once he got to the beach, he would insist on playing fetch until he or Dr. Thomson dropped dead. And he wasn't the one who was going to drop first.

And did I mention that Rudy was at war with their neighbor? This neighbor was a Vietnam veteran, a Cherokee from the hills of North Carolina, and a laid-off electrician, who touted around a 22-rifle in the pine woods next to the Thomsons. It seems that this neighbor fired one too many shots over Rudy's head. Rudy had him marked as an enemy. Every time the Thomsons pulled into the driveway with Rudy in the car, he jumped out and headed straight for that neighbor, baring his teeth. The neighbor, showing no fear, said, "I can kill him in a minute."

The Thomsons were in a dilemma. What to do with Rudy? Sooner or later, there would be an all-out confrontation. Fate solved the problem for them in a very unusual way. Late one afternoon Mrs. Thomson was out front with Rudy, when a black man from the country drove by slowly, taking a good long look at Rudy. He stopped his pickup in front of their house and said, "Sure be a nice dog. I'ze been done lookin' for one like that."

After the conversation continued for awhile, it dawned on Mrs. Thomson that this might be the answer to their dilemma. So she asked the man, "Do you want our dog?"

"Really?" he replied, dumbfounded.

Jenny turned to Rudy and asked, "Do you want to go with this man?"

At that, Rudy jumped into the back of his old pickup truck, wagging his tail, and barking, as the two rode off to the country near Andrews. The Thomsons heard later that Rudy loved his job of guarding Earl's landscaping tools. You can picture him now, driving around in Earl's pickup all day, barking at everything that moves, even the shadows.

With that, Charlie was the only dog left in their household.

Chapter Eight

Life on the Beach

Winter passed into spring and spring into summer. Heather had made it through her first year of high school. But it was rough. She was a Yankee, which some of the Southerners let her know in no uncertain terms. And she was tall and gangly, taller than all the guys in her class. She had long legs, which was why she was so good in soccer. Her face wasn't pretty. It was rather flat and featureless. Actually, the guys would have called her ugly, but no one was that unkind. Her brown hair never curled like she wanted it to. And her body wasn't taking shape like she wanted it to. She didn't have any boyfriends, or any real girl friends, for that matter. Sure, her parents were there and they loved her. But parents are parents. She needed a friend.

In the summer after her freshman year, she turned 15 and got her driver's license. That's right. In South Carolina a person can drive at the age of 15. Scary thought. Anyway, Heather's dad got her a used VW bug—an old yellow convertible. Although everything else in her life looked bleak and barren, she was thrilled to have her license, a car, and her best buddy, Charlie.

The two of them, every morning, could be seen on the beach together. Heather ran and Charlie ran. Through the shallow waters, he galloped and he pranced. She loved hearing the sound of his feet scampering in the waters. Like watery drums. Like horses. Like angels touching earth. Smooth, rapid. She would run and run, her long legs in the cool sea, taking each new flush of wave burst astride.

And Charlie ran beside her. No leash. No guns. No chasing anything. Exploding onto the beach, into the shallow sea, was Charlie. Was life. So alive. The verve was contagious. Heather laughed and laughed. And so did Charlie. She held her side, both from running too much and from laughter. She called out, holding her hands out, "Hey, Charlie. Come here, boy." She dropped to her knees and hugged him, then got back up again and took off. Charlie circled her, ran ahead, ran back. Sleek and fast, faster than the breaking waves.

When they tired of running, Heather threw a stick into the sea, and Charlie would take off after it. Head held high, he mounted each oncoming wave, paddling furiously over the whitewash, sliding down the backside of the wave, until he got deeper and deeper, where he would go to the stick, grab it decisively, then return, body surfing the waves, until he reached the place where his feet could touch sand. Then he ran to shore, stick held high in the air, as though he were a majorette displaying a baton. He pranced, he danced, then he returned the stick to Heather, who flung it out to sea again, just beyond the breakers, where Charlie would again give chase. Charlie could do this for hours. And Heather didn't mind letting the time go by. She really had nothing else to do or anywhere to go.

Often she would watch both Charlie and the surfers take some waves. As she did, a desire started to grow in her. She wanted to learn how to surf. *Why not?* she thought. *Why can't girls surf?* After Charlie's last wave in, Heather and he walked back to the car. "Hey, Charlie," she told him, "I'm gonna learn how to surf." That was cool with Charlie. He was having the time of his life. As long as he was with Heather and could go to the beach, he was in dog heaven.

Later that day, she told her mom and dad about her new desire: "I wanna learn how to surf."

Her parents were a little leery, but they knew that she was struggling to find contentment in life. So they agreed to buy her a surfboard. "Do you want some lessons?" her father asked.

"Sure."

The next day they went to HangTen Surfshop, where a muscular, tanned young man (about 18 or 19) named Jake helped her find a board that suited her size and was good for beginners. Then Mrs.

Thompson asked Jake if he would teach Heather how to surf. Heather blushed, told her mother not to ask, but was glad she did anyway. Jake agreed. "Sure. Are Tuesdays and Thursdays, 8 a.m. at the pier, okay?"

"Cool. Charlie and I are there everyday anyway."

"Who's Charlie?" he asked.

"Her dog," Mrs. Thomson replied.

"My friend," Heather said.

Heather was so excited she couldn't stand it. All that day she practiced lying on the floor and springing up to her feet in a surfer's position. Charlie liked it that she was always getting down to his level on the floor. He thought this was a new game, but he didn't understand his part in it. So he just ran around her in circles.

On the morning of the first lesson, the skies were overcast, and the waves were thigh high (about two feet) and glassy. They were perfect for learning. The first lesson, however, took place on land, where Jake taught Heather how to jump up to a surfer's position. Since she had been practicing this, she had a head start.

"Good. You got it together," Jake told her, as a bright smile spread across his tanned face.

"Been practicing," she said with a silly grin.

He adjusted the position of her feet on the board, and demonstrated how she needed to bend her knees and use her arms for balance. Then he went out with her into the water. Charlie followed right along. Jake didn't mind. "As long as he don't scratch me with his claws, it's cool with me," he told her.

Charlie swam around while Heather got on her board. When Charlie got too close, Heather would gently push him away, "No. Charlie. Stay away." And he did—for the most part. Jake, doing the scissors kick, held her board from the back, helping her to get her balance. That was the hardest part—keeping her balance. Once she got the feel for this, Jake told her, "Okay. I'm gonna send you off. Stay on your stomach the whole way in—just to get the feel of the wave moving."

In a few moments, a nice smooth wave headed their way. He shoved her off, and watched her ride it in all the way to the shallows.

All smiles, she got off her board, then waded it back into waist-deep waters. Jake met her there, and then helped her back into deeper waters. Charlie paddled along. "This time, I want you to go to your knees and keep your balance." She did it and did well. They repeated this two more times. Then he told her, "And now you're gonna try going to your feet."

Her heart was racing with fear and excitement. He got her board lined up for a nice wave, moving slightly to the right. He shoved her into the wave, holding down the back end of the board for a second, so she wouldn't pearl (that is, so the nose of the board wouldn't dip into the water causing her to flip). As soon as she felt the thrust of the wave behind her, she pushed up and got to her feet, where she held her position on the board for two seconds before falling over. When she got out of the water, Jake was hootin'. And she hooted, too. Those were some awesome two seconds. Two seconds—especially for a beginning surfer—is a long time! Charlie liked all the excitement. So he threw in a few barks.

Jake thought about her trying a few more waves, but the hour was up. He needed to get to the surf shop, and she needed to end the session on a good note.

"Good session, Heather. We'll try some more on Thursday."

"I'm stoked," she said. Then she awkwardly gave the surfer's sign (thumb and last finger out, with middle three fingers in), which Jake returned—that broad smile spreading across his tanned face again.

As Heather drove home, her head was somewhere else. She was dreamy. She was in love—no, not with Jake—but with the whole new adventure. She went home and told her mother all about the surf session. Her mom said, "I'd like to come next time."

"No way, Mom!" Heather retorted. And her mom immediately got the message.

"Okay. But remember. We have a deal. You're paying off your surfboard. Your job at the golf course starts this weekend."

"Yea. I know," she said, half-whining, half-compliant.

"We'll pay for more lessons until you get the hang of it."

Chapter Nine

Learning to Surf

The next surf lesson couldn't come soon enough for Heather. She drove to the beach an hour early and got herself ready. The waves that day were bigger than on Tuesday; there was a southeast wind about 20 miles an hour, creating surging surf, about stomach high, that was closing out quickly. As soon as each wave mounted, it broke into white surging froth, followed quickly by another wave just like it. Charlie decided to stay on shore and watch as Jake and Heather went out into the surf. Since it was high tide and the waves were choppy, Jake decided to paddle out with Heather, and give her instructions next to her, rather than wade behind her. Heather had her first lesson in paddling out against the breaking surf. It's not easy. She had to paddle hard, stay on her board, duck dive each wave as it broke, and keep paddling deeper until she got further into the sea than where the waves break. Jake kept encouraging her, "Come on, babe, you can make it!"

The "babe" part spurned her on. She didn't want to give up—not in front of Jake. So she kept paddling for all her worth. The struggle lasted about 10 minutes because she made two feet progress, then got knocked back two feet; then three feet progress, and knocked back two feet. Eventually, she came beside Jake who smiled, gave her the surfer sign, and said, "Thought you might drown, girl!"

Above the roar of the waves, she responded, "I didn't know it was this hard!"

"Yea. Surfers aren't wimps!"

The two stayed there for a few minutes, while Jake explained how she should get ready to take the wave. "Line your board slightly to the right. When I tell you when, take off paddling for all your worth. Once you feel the wave has caught you, stand up!" Jake sat on his board next to Heather, slightly behind her, holding the back of her board, until she would take off.

In a minute or so, he said, "Go," gave her a slight shove and watched her paddle. The wave went under her. He called her back into deeper waters. She made it, with difficulty, because she hadn't figured out how to turn the board around. She waited for another wave, tried again, but couldn't get it.

"You're gonna have to scoot up a bit on your board. Don't give up on the wave. Keep paddling," Jake commanded.

"Show me how."

"Okay."

Jake lined up the next good wave. Paddled hard—as if doing the free stroke—until he caught the wave. Then he jumped to his feet and rode it down the line as far the wave would go, making a few cutbacks on the way. Heather saw all this from behind and marveled how awesome it is that a person can ride along with the moving water.

When Jake paddled back to her, she congratulated him. But he said, "It's nothin'. You'll do it."

After a few more minutes, Jake got her lined up again, saw a good wave coming, gave her a shove, and shouted, "Paddle, paddle, paddle!" When he saw she got the wave, he then shouted, "Get up! Get up!" And she did. But almost as soon as she got up she fell.

Jake paddled over to where she was, and encouraged her to paddle out again. She wanted to quit, but then he said it again, "Com' on, babe, you'll get it the next time. Bend your knees when you stand up. Don't stand straight up."

With aching back and tired arms, Heather went out again. And, still, she hadn't surfed one wave. Jake lined her up once again, saw a real good wave coming, gave her a little shove, and shouted,

"Paddle, paddle, paddle!" When he saw she caught the wave, he shouted, "Get up! Get up!" And she did. This time she stood low on the board and rode the wave all the way in to shore!

Jake was shouting. Charlie was dancing in circles around Heather in the shallow waters. Heather got off her board, raised her hands, and clapped. Knowing that the session was over, Jake surfed a wave in, and congratulated Heather.

She couldn't get home fast enough to tell her mom what she did. But her mom wasn't home. So she decided to call one of her soccer buddies. She dialed the number, then hung up, thinking, *Sallie will just think I'm bragging.* So she told Charlie again and again, "I rode a wave. I rode a wave—all the way in!" She and Charlie drove back to the beach to look at the waves again, to rehearse the whole event in her mind. To somehow capture it. But one doesn't capture a ride on a wave like a mounted trophy from the sea. It is something that flows through you and can only be captured by doing it again. And even then, it can never be captured. Surfing, like creation, keeps flowing along.

That weekend Heather worked as a waitress at Seabreeze Golf Club Restaurant. It was only a weekend job because Heather was relieving a waitress who worked the weekdays. This was her first real job, so she had to put her mind to it. But her thoughts kept drifting to the beach, wondering how the waves were. Some customers came in who knew her. They were parents of a fellow soccer player. When they congratulated her on the great season, she said "thanks" but with hardly any enthusiasm. Soccer used to be her life, but things were changing now. She couldn't wait to get back in the waves.

Monday came, and there were no waves. The ocean was a pond. Tuesday came, and there was a small swell about knee high. Jake met Heather by the pier, looked at the waves, and decided to let her go out on her own. "You're all on your own, girl. I'm gonna wade out with Charlie here and watch how you do things."

Heather attached the surfleash to her right ankle, and waxed her board, which was an eight-footer. She waded out until the water was waist-high, then mounted her board, and paddled out to where the surf was starting to break. Jake called out, "You gotta paddle hard and keep paddlin' even after you catch the wave. Don't stand up right away." But Heather did exactly that, four times in a row. When she stood, the board stopped. It didn't have enough momentum. Eventually, she stayed with one wave long enough to get some speed so that when she stood up, the board kept going with the wave. She was happy, real happy, with her accomplishment. Charlie met her in the shallow surf, danced around a bit, and then ran back out into the surf and started swimming. Jake called out to Heather, "Good job, babe!" Then he called out to Charlie, "Come on out, Charlie. Come on!"

The three of them enjoyed the small surf for another half hour. Heather didn't really ride anymore waves for more than a second or two. Jake zipped down the line on three or four waves, and Charlie ran around in the shallows trying to catch minnows.

Eventually, they left the surf and walked down the beach toward the parking lot. Many heads—female heads—turned to look at Jake as he walked by. He was six feet tall, blond, blue-eyed, chiseled, with six-pack abs, gorgeous tan, bright smile, and glowing personality. Heather thought, *I know what they're thinking. 'Why is this hunk with such a plain Jane?'* Then she started laughing out loud.

"What's so funny?" Jake asked.

"Nothin'. See ya on Thursday?"

"Sure. But come early. At six, 'cause o' the tide. And tell your mom I need to get paid then."

Chapter Ten

Charlie Surfs

On the way home, Heather kept thinking of Jake's last words. *Tell your mom I need to get paid.* And then she started talking to herself. "Of course, stupid. He's not with you because you're cool. He's PAID to be with me. Oh well, whatever, you're learnin' to surf, girl, and that's what matters."

Charlie sat next to her enjoying the ride home in the VW convertible, with the breeze rushing through his hair and the sun shining on his back. He wasn't complicated like Heather. He really didn't care what Jake thought of him. All he cared was that Heather was giving him a great life. At the traffic light, she turned to stroke his head, and he leaned over to lick her face.

Heather's mom greeted them in the driveway and asked her how the session went. "Cool, it was really cool. I'm gettin' the hang of it."

"That's good, dear."

"Jake needs to be paid this Thursday."

"Sure. Do you want another week of lessons?"

"What do you think?"

"Of course, dear, one more week would be fine. Remember the week after that is soccer camp."

"Oh, yea, I forgot."

"Forgot? You've been lookin' forward to that camp for months."

"I know, Mom. Thanks for reminding me."

The next day Heather and Charlie went to the beach in the morning and the waves were like the day before. Small and glassy, about knee high. Heather took her surfboard out and Charlie followed. The tide wasn't high so she really didn't need to get on her board. When Charlie reached the depth where he had to swim, he began to paddle, nose above the water, his two front feet pumping. He kept right up with Heather as she walked her board out into the sea. When she reached five feet of water, she was just about to jump on her board, when she sensed that Charlie, right next to her, wanted to get on the board.

"Do you want to get on the board, Charlie?"

His eyes said yes. So she lifted him from behind and helped him up onto the board. His claws cut into the wax on the board, but didn't mark up the board itself. He sat with his two hind legs down underneath his body and his two front legs straight up. Heather positioned him on the board so that he would be balanced.

Then Heather sensed something else. "Charlie, do you want to surf?"

His eyes said yes.

So Heather reached down, unstrapped the leash from her right ankle, and positioned the board for a take off. She figured it would have to be a small wave, and that she would have to keep the back of the board down (just like Jake did) so that the board wouldn't pearl and Charlie flip off.

"Sure you want to surf, Charlie?"

He looked back at her with confident eyes. By now a few people had gathered at the shore to watch this event. Heather held the board still until she saw just the right wave. Then she pushed down on the back and gave the board a gentle shove. The wave caught the board just fine, and Charlie glided in all the way to shore—to the cheers of the onlookers and, most of all, to the cheers of Heather. She was so stoked she couldn't take it. She peed right there in the ocean, then swam and ran up to Charlie, giving him a big beautiful hug.

"Wanna go again, Charlie?"

He barked, spun in several circles, then headed back to the waters. Heather followed, ecstatic. She helped Charlie ride three waves that day. Minus the one wipe out, it was a super surfer session. Sure, the waves were small. But what did that matter? Charlie was stoked. Heather was stoked.

On their walk down the beach, Heather and Charlie shared a fresh kinship. They were soul mates in a new way: both could surf. Of course, they were neophytes. Grommets. But that didn't matter. They both had ridden waves.

Heather told her parents all about it. Her dad, thinking it was awesome, wanted to video Charlie surfing. Heather resisted. "No way, Dad. You're not gonna enter Charlie in some America's Funniest Animal Videos or something."

"I'd never do that without your permission," her father said.

"My permission? What does that matter? You need to ask Charlie."

The next morning Heather and Charlie met Jake at the beach where he was greeted by an outpouring from Heather: "You should have seen him, Jake!"

"Who?"

"He was surfing! Can you believe it?"

"Who?"

"Charlie! That's what I'm trying to tell you. He surfed yesterday. It was awesome."

"Cool," Jake replied. "He can do it again today."

The waves were perfect for Charlie—small and glassy. He eagerly went out with Heather and Jake. Heather helped him up on the board, where he assumed his surfer's stance: the two back legs sitting under his body, the front two legs upright. He sat there regal, like a sphinx of the ocean, mouth wide-open, hair blown by the gentle southwest breeze. When the right wave came, Heather pushed down on the back of the board and gently pushed him into the wave. The view from behind was remarkable: the back of the wave moving shoreward with a dog's silhouette moving along with it, just above the crest—until the wave crashed and spread into white foam, and the dog got off on shore. Heather was hootin' and hollerin'; so was Jake, who had never seen a dog surf before. The few people on shore who saw this also offered some shouts of joy. All around, it was a cool scene.

46

Jake went to shore, retrieved Heather's surfboard, then headed back to the deeper waters. Charlie had spotted a ghost crab, so for the moment he wasn't interested in surfing. Heather continued with her lesson, where Jake tried to teach her the concept of riding along the wall of the wave. Heather couldn't quite handle this yet; her main concentration was just on getting up and staying on the board wherever the wave took her. She enjoyed the session, which was capped off by Charlie swimming out again and riding another wave. Even though this was his fifth ride, Heather was as excited as the first. It was just too cool—her best friend, Charlie, was a surfer.

Chapter Eleven

Friends

After another week of surf lessons, Heather started to get the hang of bending her knees, riding low on her board, and directing it toward the right side of the wave, which is the easiest way for regular-footed surfers to go. (Goofy-foot surfers, who put their right forward and left foot back, like to go left.) The back foot does the steering. At her last lesson, she got a very nice ride, which an onlooker from the beach recorded on video. Actually, that onlooker was a friend of Mrs. Thomson, who was making a recording for her (since Heather didn't want her mom watching her lessons). When she parted company with Jake, he gave her a big hug, a smile, and a surfer's hand sign. She was glad to have known him, but had long ago dropped her fantasies about being his girlfriend. Still, the hug felt great!

The next week she went off to overnight soccer camp in Cary, North Carolina, and had to leave Charlie home. Charlie felt abandoned. He lay on Heather's bed with one of her shirts under his chin, looking with sad longing at the door every day, even every hour for her to return. We humans have to learn how to tell our canine friends that we are going on a trip and coming back again. It's too hard on their psyche just to be left alone with no explanation. Charlie wished Heather had told him. All he knew was that she got in someone else's car and drove away.

Dr. and Mrs. Thompson promised Heather that they would take Charlie for walks on the beach every evening. He appreciated their effort, and enjoyed romping in the shallow waves and roughing it with the other dogs. But he would look up every five minutes or so, expecting to see Heather coming down the beach. But she didn't. For Charlie, it was a long week of waiting and waiting for his favorite friend to return home.

Friday evening finally came, and so did Heather, bursting through the front door, calling out that which every dog loves to hear—their name! "Charlie! Charlie! I'm home!" Charlie burst out of her bedroom, danced in circles, jumped on her, barked, licked her face, danced in more circles, jumped on her some more, and licked her face a hundred more times. Could there be any purer joy!?

Her parents then came into the living room, hugged their daughter, welcomed her home, and started to ask a million questions about the camp. "It was good, real good. Thanks for sending me. I made some new friends. I'll tell you more later. I'm dying to go down to the beach with Charlie!" And at that, she raced out the front door, followed by Charlie, and the two drove off to the beach in her VW bug. She and Charlie enjoyed a run on the beach under the moonlight. He couldn't get enough of her. It was like a miracle to him that he hadn't been abandoned—that she really did come back. And that they were together again. Heather felt real glad, too. She had made a few new friends that week, but no one was her friend like Charlie was.

The next morning they began their usual routine of going to the beach early. She told her mother that she would never surf if she didn't do it with a friend. Things can go wrong in the water—like shark attacks, injuries from falling off the board, cramps—so it is very important to have another person nearby to help out. One of the girls Heather met at camp was Gwen. She had just moved up from Florida, was a year older than Heather, and had been surfing since she was 12. The two made an agreement to meet at the beach every morning a seven. Gwen taught Heather a lot about surfing that summer, and the two became close friends. Gwen also loved Charlie. Who wouldn't? He was so much fun to be around. And he surfed!

Anyone who saw him ride in a wave would wave and cheer. Heather and Gwen could never forget one wave that Charlie rode in all the way from about seventy-five yards out to the shallow waters. He just rode it all the way in, perfectly balanced, stepped off the board from water to land, pranced through a group of cheering onlookers and on down the shore to the next adventure. He would run and run, swim and swim, chase the migrating swarms of bluefish, follow the flow of leaping dolphins, and dally with sand crabs. He so badly wanted to catch a fish, which he did every now and again when they would get caught in the tide pools. He was so proud himself whenever he made a catch, especially the day he caught a baby shark. With fish in his soft jaw, he waved it in the sea air, as he pranced around showing everyone his trophy. He would have loved to catch a sandpiper, seagull, or pelican, but they were too fast for him.

One morning he swam right out to a brood of pelicans bobbing in the seawater. Usually, they would fly away when they saw him coming. But this time was different. When Charlie swam out there right next to them, with his head just above the water and his two front legs churning away, he didn't know what to do when he got close to them. They, so much bigger than he as they sat bobbing in the water, wouldn't budge. These were no dead ducks just lying there on top of the water ready to be grabbed up. They were big living creatures. So Charlie, kind of baffled, had to turn around and paddle back to shore.

Once he got back to the beach, he looked for the next adventure or the closest group of surfers hanging around. Charlie loved to intermingle with the surfers, as they went down the shore, into and out of the water. Heather never had to worry about him running off. No matter where she was in the water and he was on shore, he would keep an eye on her, and follow her, even if she drifted in the current. Every time she caught a wave, he would run parallel to her, and meet her in the shallows. He was as excited as she was that she had rode a wave. Charlie showed it by prancing up to Heather in the shallows, wagging his tail, beaming with pure joy. Often, he would do the same for Gwen.

When they finished their morning surf session that particular August morning, the three of them walked back to the parking lot together. As before, heads would turn—guy's heads—as the three walked by. Heather knew they weren't looking at her, but at Gwen who was a gorgeous blonde. Gwen acted as if she was used to it. "Got it all the time in Florida. The guys stare at surfer chicks," Gwen said.

"No," Heather responded quickly, "they stare at you 'cause you're drop-dead gorgeous!"

Gwen laughed it off. "So I'll see you and Charlie tomorrow morning?"

"Yea. We only got two more weeks until school. Let's enjoy every minute of it."

"That's cool."

The two weeks passed way too fast, as quick as an August wave. Before she knew it, Heather was off to school—tenth grade. The mornings were still warm and there was still enough sun to make it to the beach early in the mornings for an hour of surfing with Gwen and fun with Charlie. She had to hurry back home, shower, eat some breakfast, and rush to school, leaving Charlie all day in her room, who waited and waited for her until long past 5 p.m. because Heather went to soccer practice after school.

For Charlie, it was worth the wait because he got to spend the evening sitting with her on the bed as she studied, watched television, or talked on the phone with Gwen. He had a good life.

Chapter Twelve

Storm Coming

Heather and Gwen enjoyed being on the soccer team together. Heather got her position back as center forward, and Gwen, a junior, was the goalkeeper. The keeper from the previous year had graduated. The two would stay after practice for an extra ten to fifteen minutes to do some shooting drills—Heather shooting and Gwen trying to defend. They would laugh, joke, talk about surfing, and sometimes talk about boys, but not for too long because Heather never had a boyfriend and still didn't. By contrast, all the guys were crazy about Gwen. She was blonde, blue-eyed, with a perfect smile and figure, along with a stunning personality. Heather was amazed that Gwen would rather hang out with her than with the guys.

After taking the last practice penalty kick, the two walked off the field together as the sun was setting in the west. Heather picked up the soccer balls, and then said to Gwen, "I don't get it."

"Get what? You mean why I can't stop your p.k.'s?"

"No, I mean, I don't get it why you don't go out with guys."

"That's a no-brainer. Can't you see they just want my body? They're so shallow. They don't care for my soul. Besides, I belong to Jesus."

"What!?" Heather exclaimed, her mouth dropping wide-open.

"Yea. I belong to Jesus. Not those guys."

"What do you mean?"

"You don't know about Jesus?"

"Well, yea. But not much," Heather responded, not knowing what to make of this conversation. It was clear to her that Gwen wasn't joking. So, she dare not ask her if she was serious. But she didn't know what to make of her comments. The two said goodbye, and each went home.

Noticing how pensive Heather seemed that evening, her mother asked her, "What's on your mind?"

"Do you believe in Jesus, Mom?"

"What do you mean?"

"I mean, do you believe in Jesus?"

"Well, I believe he was an important man. And I believe he taught people to love one another. Why do you ask?"

"Well, Gwen said she belongs to Jesus, whatever that means. And I just wondered what you and Dad thought. I mean, we've never gone to church or anything. What does Dad think?"

"Well, you can ask him when he gets home."

Later that evening, when Dad came home from work, she did ask him. "Dad, what do you think about Jesus?"

"Well, I think he was like a prophet or something. People say he did some miracles. I'm not sure. Why do you ask—are you doing some kind of report or something?"

"No, just wonderin'."

The next day at school, when Heather saw Gwen, she wanted to talk about Jesus. But it was not the right place and right time. So she let it pass. That day was their first game, a scrimmage against Myrtle Beach High School. Both their minds were focused on the game. They each did well in the scrimmage. Gwen allowed only one goal, and Heather got one goal—a penetrating strike into the upper corner. And Heather got an assist. They didn't talk much after the game, except about the game, and they didn't really talk about Jesus for a long time to come. Gwen didn't bring it up, and Heather thought she was too unlearned to ask anything intelligent.

As August passed into September, Heather kept going to the beach in the mornings with Charlie, but not always to surf, sometimes just to stroll. This was her favorite time of day—to watch the grayness slide away from the horizon like a long boarder moving down the line, to feel the sunbeams wrap around her face and body, to hear the seagull caws catch the air and waves crumble onto shore. Never before, as when she lived in Ohio, had she felt so close to nature. She would tell herself, "If this is God, then I believe." She would throw a stick for Charlie into the sea, and watch him again and again swim and fetch. The time was always too short, not like in the summer when time is as still as the sun on the eastern horizon.

Sadly, for Charlie mostly, these times were never long enough. He lived for these jaunts to the beach. The hours in between, hours when Heather was learning history or studying Spanish or practicing soccer, were vacant for Charlie. He would doze, he would dream. But the dreams were not always pleasant. Wild boars would appear and chase him. Men with shotguns would scream at him. Swamp mud would suck him down. He was running and swimming and trying to escape. Sometimes his legs were flailing. Sometimes he would yowl.

One afternoon in early September, Heather came charging into her bedroom and woke Charlie from his dreams: "Come on, boy! Come on! We gotta get out o' here! A hurricane's coming!" Charlie got to his feet, shook off his sleepiness, and was at her side immediately. Heather grabbed some of her keepsakes, photos, videos, and jewelry, and then ran out to her car in the gravel driveway. Already, the pines were bending tremendously in the force of the wind, and the palm leaves were shaking. The mid-afternoon sky was turning engine black, and the rain was falling like diving pelicans. Heather and Charlie got into the VW bug and started driving to Georgetown, where she hoped to meet her parents, both of whom worked at the Georgetown Hospital—her father as a doctor in radiology and her mother as a nurse in neo-natal care. Since everyone exiting Grand Strand had to go through Georgetown, it made sense for Heather to join her parents there and then evacuate the coastal area with them.

Going south on highway 17, otherwise known as Ocean Highway, was extremely difficult because the wind was blowing east to west with winds 60 miles an hour, gusting as high as 70. Heather was struggling to keep her car on the highway. She couldn't exceed 30 miles an hour and keep control. With windshield wipers swiping like madmen and impatient drivers passing her, Heather was holding the wheel with all her might, bracing against the gusts. Her mind was racing. *Should I turn around and go home? Have my parents already left?* Then she nervously spoke to Charlie sitting next to her, "What should we do?" He looked at her with a blank expression and then turned his head to look out the window on his side. By now all the pine trees were bending like fully bent pole vaults, and some of them were starting to snap.

After what seemed an eternity, she reached the stretch of highway just before the first bridge, which crosses the Wacammaw River. When she got about one hundred feet before the bridge, a huge gust came out of the southeast and blew her car off the road. She lost control and slid down the embankment leading down to the river. The car bounced off several pine trees on the way down, then flipped over and over until it came to a standstill, right side up, about 20 yards from the raging, wind-whipped river.

Charlie had been thrown up against the window and suffered severe lacerations to his head and shoulder. Heather was unscathed because she was wearing a seatbelt. Nonetheless, she was in shock and couldn't move.

Chapter Thirteen

Survival

Eventually, Heather came out of her shock because Charlie started whining. She unlatched her belt, took off her shirt, ripped it in strips, and started soaking up the blood on Charlie's head and shoulder, who lay next to her on the passenger seat. "Oh, Charlie. Charlie. I'm so sorry, Charlie."

Heather tried to roll down her window to check out their situation, but it was as if they were in a heavy carwash. She had no choice but to just sit there. Fortunately, they were down in a ravine, nearly under the bridge. So the main force of wind was passing over them. Nonetheless, the car was still rocking. Heather got out for a quick moment and saw that they were quite close to the river, which freaked her out. She feared that a wind gust would blow them into the river or the water would rise and sweep them away. She was right about one thing: the water was rising.

"Charlie," she whined, "we can't stay in here much longer. River's rising." She thought they might have a chance of walking up the hundred yard long embankment up the road and getting help. So she got of the car and helped Charlie out. But when she tried to walk against the wind, it was impossible. Rather, the wind torrents kept knocking her down. She had no choice but to crawl on her knees toward the pines behind her on the west. Charlie followed as best he could. These pines stood about ten feet above the river and thirty yards back.

With herculean effort and desperate grunts, Heather made it to the edge of the pines and then crawled interiorly another twenty yards where she found an indentation. Charlie did the same. She sat with her bare back against a pine tree, having given up her shirt for Charlie's wounds. And she had Charlie sit under her bent legs, with his head on her lap, so that she could tend to his wounds.

The two huddled there, fearfully watching the tall pines bend nearly to the ground, hearing some of them snap, fall, and crash. The two huddled there, with rain pelting them and branches whipping them, especially on Heather's back. The two huddled there, as the wind increased in speed, and the hurricane came to shore, like a wheel within a wheel, circling furiously fast, pushing time backward to a heart-pounding halt, as an unmanned engine sped by, a sea-sucking funnel whirling fury everywhere. Heather was terrified. She had never been in a hurricane. And this one was awesome.

She prayed, *O God, we don't want to die. Don't let Charlie and me die.*

In a few minutes the fury faded, the rain subsided, and they could see some clouds being penetrated by the western sun. "Thank God!" she sighed out loud. As the pines started to straighten, she stood up, stretched her body, took some deep breaths, and started to relax. The forest was still dripping with wetness, and the ground beneath them was soaking wet. They walked to the edge of the brim and overlooked the river, which had gotten much wilder, wider, and higher—about seven feet up the ten feet embankment. She looked over at her VW bug which was now in two feet of water, and the water was winning. Heather panicked, thinking she had to save her car. But then she knew it was no use. So she thought they could make it back up the other long embankment to the road and get help.

They started to make the climb, but the water running down the embankment was too fierce and was deepening. They had no choice but to go back into the woods where they were before. As they did, they started to get hit by the backside of the hurricane, which bent the trees in the other direction and poured truckloads of rain from the sky, which was jet-black again. Heather resumed her previous position of placing her back against a pine tree, this time on the opposite side to shield herself and Charlie from the counterclockwise winds now whirling from the northwest. After another hour of this onslaught, the waters from the river reached the top of the embankment, so Heather and Charlie had to hurry to get deeper into the woods. Fortunately, they found a fallen oak which was leaning up against a cluster of sturdy pines on an angle that enabled Heather to climb it. Before she made the climb, she picked up Charlie and put him on a crow's nest—a place where two huge branches joined. Then she climbed up.

They had to stay there like that the whole night, while the waters beneath them rose. Eventually, the hurricane changed to a storm and the storm to a drizzle. In the morning there was sunshine and two feet of water beneath them. Heather looked at Charlie and saw that he was still bleeding in one laceration, so she took the strips off him, wrung out the blood, and tied them around him again. This didn't work, so she took off her shorts, ripped them in pieces, tied them in one long swath, and wrapped it around Charlie's wound. He had lost a lot of blood and looked half dead. The light had left his eyes. Heather was fearful for his life. She picked him up and held him near the water and encouraged him to drink. He took a few sips, nothing more. So Heather cupped her hands and took in some water; she put her mouth down to the water and lapped it in. "Com' on, Charlie, you can do it."

Charlie took some long drinks, and then some more, which gladdened Heather's heart and lightened it a bit. She picked up Charlie and started walking through the woods back toward the highway, hoping someone would be out driving. But the road was too inundated with water for driving. She found a large plank, which she placed Charlie on, and headed up highway 17 in waist deep water, pushing him ahead of her. All along the way, she had to weave around fallen pines, and push aside fallen branches. Their only source of energy came from drinking the water, which was somewhat brackish. After four hours of walking like this, Heather came to Hobcaw Barony, a research institute for marine biology situated on the coastal marshlands. She entered the driveway, and made it up the door of the main building. It was obvious that it had been evacuated. Heather broke open the front door by smashing in the window with a board and reaching for the inside handle.

Once inside, she looked for some food, and found some bottled water and peanut butter crackers, which she shared with Charlie. Then she found some needle and thread, having made the horrendous decision to sew up Charlie's wound—at least, the real bad one. But once she laid Charlie down and tried to make the first puncture, he cried out and jumped up. So she tried to find any bandages she could, and fortunately found a first-aid kit. She applied antibiotics, put bandages all over Charlie, and wrapped gauze all around him. Then she looked for some clothes and found a tank top swimming suit in the bathroom. She also found a dry towel, which she used on herself first, though quite sparingly. Then she wrapped it around Charlie. The two of them lay down on the tile floor in a position where Heather could keep applying pressure to Charlie's one bad wound.

It would be an entire day and another night before the waters would subside enough for cars to drive on highway 17. The next morning, one employee came into the building, saw the two lying there, and thought they were dead.

"Hey," Heather said. "We've been through hell. Sorry about the door."

"No problem," the young man answered.

"Gotta get Charlie here to a vet. He's lost lots of blood."

"I'll call. Don't think any vets are open. But I do know a guy in Georgetown who has a clinic in his house."

"Pleaaaaase—take us there now."

Within minutes, they were on their way. The vet, Dr. Smith, saw that Charlie needed a blood transfusion. He called some vets in Charleston that could do this.

"Can ya'll fetch him down to Charleston now?"

"My car drowned. But I'll call my parents at Georgetown Hospital."

Chapter Fourteen

Saving Charlie

On the way to Charleston, Dr. Thomson drove as fast as he could without going 10 miles over the speed limit. In the back seat, Mrs. Thomson held up a bag of solution which was running an IV into Charlie's vein, who was sitting next to Charlie. Heather, nervous and hyper, went on and on about the whole ordeal, telling her parents everything and then some. They didn't even have to ask one question.

"We thought you were at home during the hurricane," Mrs. Thomson said, her voice cracking under the strain of it all. "We called once, but then the phone lines went dead."

Dr. Thomson broke in: "We had no idea it would become a level three—almost four. And so quickly! We thought we had till midnight."

"Dad, I'm sorry. I was trying to get to you guys. The car's gone. Lost. Drowned forever."

"It's okay, honey. You're alive. That's what matters."

"What matters is that Charlie lives," Heather said. "I'm fine, Dad. Pleeeeaaassse—go faster!"

"If I go any faster, the cops will stop me."

"But it's an emergency!"

Soon they were speeding past Awendaw at 80 miles an hour. "This is where I first found Charlie," Mrs. Thomson remarked. No one said anything in response, as all their thoughts turned to Charlie and what a wonderful companion he had become to them. Silence ruled as Dr. Thomson headed into Mt. Pleasant and neared the veterinary hospital. The only sound in the car was Charlie's labored breathing. Soon they reached the hospital.

"Oh my goodness!" Mrs. Thomson blurted out. "This is the same vet I took Charlie to before!"

"Good," Heather answered, "then they'll take good care of him." And they did.

Charlie spent the day and night at the clinic, having received a blood transfusion, more nutrients through an IV, and special care from an extraordinary vet, Dr. Randall. Heather and her mother waited and eventually slept in the waiting room, while Dr. Thomson helped Dr. Randall with various procedures, such as stitching Charlie's wounds.

Dr. Randall came out into the waiting room around two in the morning. His voice sounded exhausted but relieved. "Charlie's gonna make it!"

"Thank God!" Heather said, who got up from the floor and threw her arms around him. And then she hugged her daddy when he came out of the room, looking just as exhausted but also relieved.

"Ya'll should check into the hotel down yonder. Get some sleep. Charlie's got angels lookin' out for him. I called my assistant. She'll come in to stay with him all night. See ya in the mornin'," the vet said on his way out the door.

When they came to get Charlie the next day, Dr. Randall gave them all the particulars for Charlie's care. Then he gave Dr. Thomson the bill of $880. "Sorry, folks. Gotta charge ya this time."

"How 'bout my fee?" Dr. Thomson joked, then said seriously, "No problem. We'll send you a check tomorrow."

When they got back home, they put Charlie on Heather's bed, and then they started to deal with the damage to their property. Three of their back windows were blown out completely. A pine tree had fallen on their back porch, gashing a hole in the roof. Pine trees and palm trees were down everywhere on their acre of land. The water had obviously come as high as their back door and seeped into their kitchen. Overwhelmed, Mrs. Thomson started to cry. Heather consoled her and then said, "Mom, I lost all my best photos, letters, and personal keepsakes. They went down in the car. But I'm not sad 'cause we made it. You and Dad made it. And Charlie made it."

"You're right, honey," Mrs. Thomson said, as she dried her tears with a towel. "Let's clean up this mess."

As they worked, they listened to the radio broadcaster talking about the disaster. The entire coast of northeastern South Carolina and southern North Carolina from Georgetown up to Wilmington had been hit with hard winds and heavy rains. By comparison with some of the houses they heard about—houses that had been completely blown apart—the Thomsons considered themselves fortunate.

Heather looked in on Charlie every 10 minutes or so and saw that he was sleeping well. He was still hooked up to an IV, taking in nutrients and antibiotics. Charlie was dreaming of the beach, of chasing pelicans and swimming with dolphins. He was dreaming of endless sun warming his bones. When Heather saw him shaking, she covered him with her blanket, and sat beside him stroking his head. She spoke softly to him, "Charlie, you're gonna make it. We're gonna surf again, boy."

Gwen came over to visit that evening, and she and Heather exchanged stories. Gwen's story was nothing like Heather's story. When Gwen heard of Heather's journey, she said, "No way! You lost your car? You and Charlie spent the night in the woods? And you broke into a marine biology building? Sounds like a cool movie."

"Believe me, Gwen. It was more than scary. I thought Charlie was going to die."

"Can I see him?" Gwen asked.

"Sure. He'd love to see you."

When Gwen went in and Charlie saw whom she was, he wagged his long tail, flapping it on the bed as if it were a mallet on a big bass drum. The two girls gloated over him and praised him for several minutes, calling him the best dog in the world many times over, promising him endless beach and surf. He loved it.

Heather and Gwen checked the surf the next morning. It was a lot smaller than they imagined and the ocean was pushed back about 100 feet from where it would normally be. The northwest wind was on it, the back side of the hurricane, making small little tubes. They went out, caught some fun rides, and enjoyed a beautiful morning in late September. The ocean was still warm, and the sky, washed with rain, was brilliantly blue.

The storm over, the weekend over, and fear for Charlie's recovery over, Heather felt it was anticlimactic to go back to school on Monday. Gwen gave her a ride that day and for the next two weeks, until Heather could get a new set of wheels—another used VW bug, replaced by the insurance money for the other one. Heather and Gwen joked at length about her drowning car, affectionately calling it the "dead bug" and "the drowned beetle."

Soccer practice started up again, as did the season. Heather had to get her spirits in groove again, as well as her body. She was sore from the whole ordeal, a lot sorer than she thought. After soccer practice, many of girls on the team, having heard about Heather's experience, wanted to know how she was doing. Because Heather had become vulnerable, she had become approachable. In their eyes, she was no longer just the superstar Yankee. She was a regular girl. And they all wanted to know how Charlie was doing. By now, everyone knew how inseparable Heather and Charlie had become.

Chapter Fifteen

Soccer and More Soccer

Heather got back in the groove again with soccer. She recovered her touch on the ball. It felt good. Her best sense of satisfaction was just passing the ball back and forth with some teammates, feeling and hearing the soft thud of the ball on the instep of her foot. There's just something about soccer. The white ball moving around on the bright green field, being passed between players. It brings a kind of connectedness, a fluid unity among those so engaged. It's sweet. Those who play it know. She felt good, all the way down into the deep part of her soul.

Heather was in the mood to play. She got the starting position again as a forward. Some call it "striker," because that was her primary function on the team—to the strike the ball on goal, to smack it into the back of the net. If a striker is "on," she is "on." If she's "off," she's "off" and the whole team suffers. In a soccer game, a lot of team play goes into moving the ball forward, just to get it into scoring position. A team may get only 12 to 15 chances in a game to make a shot on goal. The shots have to count. So there's a lot of pressure on the forwards. But they can't feel that pressure or they'll get too tense. And they have to have a good vibe with the team and know that the team is with them whether they score or not. But strikers can't be cocky and think they are the most important member of the team when they've scored. "Hi-fives" have to go all around. It's a delicate psychological game within the game, and Heather was learning how to play it.

Gwen was the starting goalkeeper. She had a great sense about the game and where to position herself and when. She had lots of practice trying to stop Heather's shots during and after practice. The two enjoyed their camaraderie. But during a game they were usually on opposite ends of the field. Nonetheless, they pulled for each other in their hearts. Gwen got excited every time she saw Heather with the ball, and she would always run the length of the field to hug her when she scored—and then quickly run back to goal to get ready for the next kick-off. Heather got really jazzed when Gwen made a save—and though she couldn't run back to hug her (because play continued), she'd give Gwen a beaming smile and the surfer's sign.

Their enthusiasm—from front to back—was contagious. All the team members got into it. The team was for the team. They talked to each other during the game, shouted out compliments, and held their tongue when someone screwed up. This team spirit really helped because, since their team had won the regional championship the year before, all their opponents were out to get them. They couldn't become their own nemesis.

In the first game of the season, they met their arch rivals from Charleston. The score was 0-0 at half time. Both teams had a solid defense, and neither team was shooting well on the few chances they had. The score stayed that way until the last ten minutes, when Charleston scored off a corner kick and quick volley. There was nothing Gwen could do to save it. With three minutes left to go, Heather made a run in the opponent's box, got a good pass, and was just about to take a shot on goal, when her feet were swept out from underneath her by a defender. She lay on the field for several minutes, trying to catch her breath, and then was taken off the field, while the rest of her team got ready for a penalty kick. Sandra, the other forward, took the kick—low to the keeper's left side—and scored. The game ended with a 1-1 tie. The coach and team were satisfied with the result because a come-from-behind draw feels like a victory.

Heather nursed her wound (on her left calf) for the next couple of days, spending her afternoons and evenings with Charlie. The two walked together slowly around the back yard and looked at the blue jays and cardinals swoop from tree limb to limb, and then they went to the pond in the back to look for alligators and turtles. An alligator visited their pond every month or so, and then would move on to another pond to do his fishing. The turtles were always there, except in the dead of winter, poking their heads just above the water's surface or sunning on the bank of the pond. Heather was glad to see that Charlie was recovering, but she worried that he was so skinny. "Gotta eat more, Charlie. I'm gonna get ya some steak."

The next game came too soon for Heather's leg, but she played anyway. Thankfully, it was an easier team, so Heather found herself unmarked by the defense on more than one occasion and was able to get off some clean shots. She scored two goals, which was good enough to give her team a 2-0 victory. In the following two games, Heather found herself in the box yet again and again, unmarked and ripping shots. She scored lots of goals. This pattern changed in the next two games, however, because she was being double-teamed. Nonetheless, she became a play maker, feeding perfect, crisp passes to Sandra, who scored two goals in each of the games. Heather enjoyed assisting on goals just as much as scoring them. This attitude pumped up the team.

The sixth game, against Myrtle Beach, was nerve-racking. The teams were evenly matched, and both goalkeepers were hot. Good shots didn't end up in the back of the net. The score was 0-0 until the last five minutes, when Myrtle Beach scored off a fluke deflection on a corner kick. The girls were pretty bummed out, even all the way home on the bus ride. The coach was cool about it; she told the team it could have gone either way.

That night Heather lay down in bed, with Charlie right next to her. He could sense her sadness. He kept nuzzling up to her, pushing her arms from underneath so that they would get into action—the action of petting him. Then he rolled over on his back for his favorite of all—the tummy scratch. There in the darkness of her bedroom they comforted each other—Heather, for her loss, and Charlie, for his loneliness, since school and soccer took Heather away for nearly the whole day. Heather was glad that tomorrow was Saturday. Before going to sleep, she told him, "Hey, Charlie, tomorrow morning we're going to the beach." He loved that word, "beach." It was his favorite word in all the world. He liked it even better than "num-num," which is code for "dog food."

The next morning they went to the beach and were greeted by gorgeous chest-high waves, peeling in from the south. Heather was soon joined by Gwen, and the two paddled out to catch some waves. The paddle-out was quite difficult for them, especially for Heather, but they both eventually made it beyond the white breakwater. Charlie stayed in the shallows and watched the event. Both girls caught the same wave, and both rode it together, down the line, hootin' and hollerin', just like the guys. For Heather, it was the best ride of her life. She took the wave all the way into shore, where she was greeted by the glee of Charlie, dancing and prancing in the shallows. She hugged him and kissed him, and threw a few sticks for him. Then she paddled out to get another, and then another. The day was a glorious day for surfers, and a glorious day for dogs. Heather and Charlie found heaven, and it was on earth.

Chapter Sixteen

Dognapped

September turned into October, but unlike in Ohio that didn't mean the leaves changed colors. In coastal South Carolina, October brings slightly cooler weather, but it is still warm. Even the ocean is still warm, warm enough to surf bareback. But the days get shorter in October. The sun comes up later and goes down sooner. So Heather could take Charlie to the beach for only a half hour each morning before school. Charlie took full advantage of his time, running to his heart's content, playing with other dogs he knew, and chasing any and every kind of bird. His new adventure was to try to catch a fish. When a school of bluefish or pinheads or spots swarmed not far from the last breaker, he would swim out and chase the moving mass of popping silver flash, but was never able to snag one. Heather would have to go into the water and coax him to get out with ardent fervency before he would obey.

Charlie never wanted to leave the beach, nor did Heather. But she had to get to school, where studies awaited her, as well as soccer. Her sophomore year was not as bad as her freshman year. She had made some friends, especially the girls on the soccer team, and especially Gwen. But Gwen had so many guys after her that the only time Heather saw her was during soccer practice or during a game. As far as Heather knew, not even one guy looked at her with even the slightest hint of attraction. She was still gangly and very plain. The only comments she would ever get from guys came from some varsity players on the men's soccer team congratulating her on a goal or something she did in a game.

Lots of kudos would come in the next three weeks because Heather got on a roll. She scored two hat tricks in the next two games, and two goals each in the following two games. Added to this, she had five assists. The team was rocking and rolling, sure to get a top seed in the state championship. They had three more games to play, and then the playoffs would begin.

After a Wednesday practice, Heather had to go into Georgetown to get some new shin guards. Of course, she took Charlie along, who loved to ride in the car, especially when she had the top down. Just outside Georgetown near the two bridges there's a Taco Bell. Heather pulled in to get some chaluppas. When she saw that the line for the drive through was pretty long, she decided to go inside to get quicker service. Besides, she had to use the bathroom. She parked her VW bug and told Charlie to wait while she went inside. "I'll get ya some water," she told him. While Heather went into Taco Bell, Charlie enjoyed the cool breeze coming off Winyah Bay.

Duke, Bo's relative, pulled up in his pickup truck and parked right next to Heather's car. He took one look at Charlie and called out, "Hey, Champ! How ya doin'?"

Charlie looked over at him, as though he recognized the voice.

"I thought you was lost," Duke said, as he got out of his truck and walked up to Charlie. "But now you're back." Duke grabbed Charlie, turned back toward his truck, and was putting him in the front cab of his truck just when Heather came out of Taco Bell and saw what was happening. She screamed, "You can't steal my dog!" and ran toward the truck. Duke put the truck in reverse, revved the engine and ran into her, sending her flying backwards.

Though she was badly hurt and bleeding, adrenaline took over. She quickly got into her car and sped after the truck, following him all the way to his house on the outskirts of Georgetown toward Andrews. When he pulled into the driveway, she pulled in after him. She jumped out of her car, ran over to Charlie, grabbed him in her arms and headed back to her car.

"Don't you take another step!" Duke's voice boomed, "Or I'll blow your cockin' head off."

Heather turned and saw this redneck pointing a shotgun straight at her head. "He's my dog!" she shot back.

"No he ain't. Was my cousin's. He's Bo's dog."

"He's my dog!" Heather insisted.

"Bo's gone. I reckon he's my dog now!"

Holding Charlie close to her, Heather whispered in his ear with all fervency, "Run, Charlie. Run!" Then she turned toward her car and let him go, shielding him as long as she could. Charlie took off at breakneck pace, weaving between some pine trees. The hotheaded redneck lost it. He turned his rifle toward Charlie, took aim, and was just about to squeeze the trigger when he got jolted by Heather who kicked him with her hardest kick right into his scrotum. As he bent over in pain, she ran back to her car, went in reverse, then forward, and started to head down the road after Charlie. All of a sudden, she heard his rifle fire twice, and her car went into a spin. He had hit her back tires. With a further spurt of adrenaline and quick thinking, she grabbed her keys, jumped from the car and ran into a nearby woods.

Dusk was giving way darkness, so she really didn't have much to go on other than she knew which way was east. She dare not call out to Charlie, for that would give away her position. So she just kept heading east for about half an hour. But then it dawned on her that Charlie might come back to the car. And she was right. He did. Duke was there to get him.

By the time Heather made her way back to the car, it was pitch dark. A new moon, like a sliver of fingernail, gave off some faint light, but not much. Heather crawled underneath her car and waited all night for Charlie to return.

When Heather didn't get home by nine, and then by ten, her parents started calling some of her friends. Gwen knew that she had gone into Georgetown to buy some shin guards. So the Thompsons called the Georgetown police, then got into their car and spent the whole night driving around Georgetown searching for Heather. They didn't find her, and the police didn't find her.

Before the first morning light, Heather crawled out from beneath her car, walked over to Duke's house and noticed that his truck was gone. She heard some dogs barking in the back, but discovered they were bloodhounds. She opened Duke's back door, went into the kitchen and called 9-1-1. The police arrived in 10 minutes, and her parents arrived a few minutes later, after having been contacted by the police on Dr. Thomson's cell phone.

Heather was hysterical: "He stole Charlie! He stole him! He took him somewhere. I tried to save Charlie, but that redneck tried to kill him. He tried to kill me, too. He shot my car full of holes."

Mrs. Thomson held Heather's hand, trying to console her, while Dr. Thomson and the police tried to put together the events. Heather blurt out in rapid succession the entire story. "I was at Taco Bell. Went in to get some food. This redneck pulls up and takes Charlie into his truck. Drives off. I follow him to his house here. I grab Charlie. He aims his shotgun at my head. Claims Charlie was his cousin's dog. Threatens to kill me. When Charlie runs off, he tried to shoot him. But I kicked him in his you-know-where. When I tried to drive off, he shot at me! Look at my car! I waited all night for Charlie to come back," she sobbed. "We gotta look for him."

One of the policemen asked, "You got any proof that's your dog?"

"Whose side are you on, anyway?!" Heather retorted.

"Your side," he responded, holding up his hands as if to say, "Cool it."

The other policeman said, "We'll camp out here till this guy gets back. Believe me, no matter what's the deal with the dog—"

"His name is Charlie," Heather interrupted.

"Okay, okay. No matter what's the deal with Charlie, we're gonna arrest this man for attempted murder."

"Look at my back. Look at the bump on my head. He ran me over in the parking lot at Taco Bell. He's a madman. Mom and Dad, we gotta look for Charlie."

"We'll help you," one of the officers said, "once we get some others in here to stake off the crime scene, get some photos, and all

71

that stuff. Gotta leave your car right there. And sorry, ya'll gotta come down to headquarters to answer some questions."

"I gotta look for Charlie! That's what I gotta do!" Heather demanded.

"Of course, but we need a statement from you and we need to have a doctor examine you."

"My dad's a doctor."

"That's good, but we need another doctor to write up a report."

Heather knew that time was a wastin', so she complied by going down to headquarters. After this, she got some coffee, her parents got some coffee, and the three spent the day driving through the parts of Georgetown where they might find him. They drove and drove until dark. Heather called his name out again and again—"Charlie, Charlie"—until her voice was hoarse.

They went home exhausted and depressed.

Chapter Seventeen

The Search

Charlie was not in Georgetown. Nowhere close. The night Duke stole him he had taken Charlie with him on a drive down to the Francis Marion Woods, to go to Lake Guillard. He left about four in the morning while Heather was still sleeping underneath her car. Ever since Bo's sudden disappearance or mysterious death, there had been a $10,000 reward for solid information leading to an arrest. Duke hoped Charlie—whom he called Champ—could lead him to Bo's body.

Charlie was very nervous being in the truck with Duke. He started shaking and couldn't stop. "What's wrong with you, boy!?" Duke yelled at him. "You sure is skinny. No wonder you're shakin'." Then he slapped Charlie on the side of his head. When they got to Bo's favorite hunting spot near Lake Guillard, it was dawn. Duke had Charlie on a leash, and was yanking him this way and that, just about choking him to death, as he directed Charlie here and there, constantly commanding him, "Where's Bo? Got get Bo." Charlie didn't care where Bo was. He had had nothing to drink for nearly a day and was extremely thirsty. So he headed for the lake, even while being choked, as Duke yanked back on the leash, not letting him go there. Charlie turned the direction Duke wanted him to go for a minute or so, then tried to get to the lake again. Duke took the handle end of the leash and whipped Charlie, shouting at him, "You do as I say, you skinny runt!" He whipped and whipped him until he started bleeding. Charlie yelped, turned around, and showed his fangs. Duke kept yanking on him and was about to whip again, when Charlie gathered all his strength, lunged on Duke, throwing him backwards to the ground, then bit him in the neck with the full force of his jaws, severing his jugular vein. Then Charlie ran to the lake, took a long drink, then headed off into the woods.

Charlie had been in this woods before, and he had survived there before. So he determined to do the same again, until he could find Heather.

Heather woke up the next morning in pain. Her entire body was stiff and soar beyond belief. The adrenaline gone, she felt every bruise on her back and her neck. More than that, she felt the loss of Charlie. She wanted to get out of bed quickly, to run to her car, and go out a look for Charlie. But her body wouldn't cooperate and she had no car. She cried out in pain as she moved slowly toward the bathroom, "O God! Where's Charlie?"

Hearing her groans, her mom came to her aide and tried to console her.

"We gotta look again, Mom."

"I know, honey. But we've got to get you to a doctor first."

"Dad's a doctor. I just need some pain medication. Have him call it in to the Georgetown CVS. Let's go."

Knowing how desperate Heather was, Mrs. Thomson wasn't about to argue. They spent that entire day looking for Charlie, but to no avail. Heather's team had a soccer game that day, but it didn't even cross her mind. As they drove around the old city of Georgetown, Mrs. Thomson told her, "I called your coach and told her that you had been hit by a truck and were quite bruised."

"Thanks, Mom. I hadn't even thought of soccer."

"I know."

"Did you tell her about Charlie?"

"No."

"Why not?"

"What was I supposed to say?"

"Do you think we'll find him?" Heather asked sadly.

"Sure, dear. Charlie's got angels."

"Yea. Angels. And he's an angel. He can get out o' any hell."

But they didn't find him that day. Many calls to the police department produced the same thing. No one had seen Charlie.

The next two days were Saturday and Sunday. Heather and her friend Gwen spent the entire weekend putting up posters all around Georgetown, posters with Charlie's picture on it, offering a $500 reward for his return. They walked up and down the boardwalk in historic Georgetown, talking to as many as people as they could, showing them the picture of Charlie. They met a lot of nice folk, but no one had seen Charlie. He was unique among golden retrievers in that he was smaller and much thinner than the usual retriever, and he had a touch of red running through his blond hair. Plus, he had scars on his stomach and on his shoulder. No one had seen a dog that matched that description.

Monday came around and Heather had to face the reality of going to school again and going to soccer. She knew the team would be counting on her for the next two games. They had lost miserably in the game she didn't play in. But she had no heart for soccer. She didn't even have any will. After school, instead of going to soccer practice, she drove her car (now fixed) into Georgetown to look for Charlie. When she came back, long after dark, her mother greeted her at the door. She knew where Heather had been, so there was no need to ask.

"When the coach called, I covered for you. I told her you were still in bad pain."

"That's true. I'm aching. And my heart is breaking. Tell her that. 'Cause I'm not going to school or to soccer or anywhere until I find him!"

"Honey. You gotta keep doing your life."

"No! There is no life without Charlie." And with that Heather went into her bedroom and slammed her door shut.

After a very bad, sleepless night, Heather took off early in the morning to go to Georgetown. She went back to Duke's house and tried to recreate in her mind what had happened that night. As she reconstructed the events, it came to her. "Of course. Charlie came back to the car while I was still in the woods. That redneck got him and took him off somewhere—somewhere way beyond Georgetown."

She went to the nearest pay phone and called the police, who came out to meet her at Duke's house. She convinced the policeman that Charlie would not be found in Georgetown. Since Duke had not returned to his house and since no one in Georgetown had reported his presence, the officer was doubly convinced.

"Where could he have gone?" Heather asked plaintively.

"Don't reckon I know, but I've got a hunch," the officer responded.

"What do ya mean?"

"Well, awhile back his cousin disappeared. Guy named Bo. Down in the Francis Marion Woods. Probably was shot. There's a $10,000 reward for information leading to an arrest. I bet Duke's after that money. He might have done gone down yonder. And takin' your dog. Didn't you say he said Charlie was his cousin's dog?"

"You're right. He did."

Heather called her parents about this new revelation. Her dad had to go to work, but her mom took another day off. She and Heather drove with the officer down to the Francis Marion Woods. The officer knew the spot where Bo had been because all the cops had talked about it ever since Bo's disappearance. When they arrived at the place, they saw a pickup truck, which Heather identified as belonging to Duke. Heather wanted to call out for Charlie, but the officer wouldn't let her in case Duke would hear them and run off. In fact, he told the two that they had to stay in the patrol car with the doors locked until he returned.

The officer headed down a trail near the lake, where eventually he saw turkey vultures circling. As he neared the place, the vultures flew off. The closer he got, he was overpowered by a horrific stench. Covering his nose, he inched his way forward until he saw the mangled remains of a corpse. He went closer to see if the corpse could be recognized at all. But the eyes and cheeks had been gouged out. He left the scene as quickly as possible, vomited, then cleared his eyes. After this, he went back to the patrol car where he radioed in the report of a dead body.

As they waited for a local sheriff to come to the scene, the Georgetown officer told the women what he saw.

"Do you think it was Duke?" Mrs. Thomson asked nervously.

"Could likely be. An autopsy report will tell us for sure. You can look for Charlie now. We got an hour before dark."

Heather wandered the area, calling out again and again, "Charlie! Charlie! Come here, Charlie!" Her mother did the same. But there was no answer and there wouldn't be. Charlie was miles away, working his way through Hellhole swamp again.

During the drive home, Heather's mom made a deal with her: "If you promise to go back to school tomorrow and play out the rest of this season for your team, I will hire a detective to find Charlie. We need an expert here."

"Okay, Mom." Heather replied, her voice despondent.

Chapter Eighteen

Still Searching

Heather went to school the next day, and she showed up for soccer practice. News had gotten out about what happened to her and what happened to Charlie. It was very distracting to the team. The coach decided it was a good thing to let her talk to the team, so they all could hear about it once and for all—and straight from Heather.

"Well, guys. Ya see. Some redneck stole Charlie while I was at Taco Bell. He tried to run me over. (Everyone laughed.) Seriously, he did. That's why I was so bruised and stiff. Sorry I wasn't at the game. Anyway, I followed this redneck to his house and—"

The coach interrupted, "How 'bout you not call him a redneck?"

"Oh, he's worst than that! (More laughs.) Anyway, when I went to his house, he threatened to kill me. Pointed his shotgun straight at my head. I helped Charlie escape by kicking that redneck—that man—in the you-know-where." Heather then demonstrated the kick. "Harder than any shot I've ever taken. Then when I tried to escape in my car, he shot the back of my car full of holes. Tried to kill me. Anyway, he's... he's gone now. And so is Charlie. And I'm—" Heather couldn't finish her sentence. She was too choked with tears, as were the rest of her teammates—and even the coach.

Once they got their composure, the coach asked them all to join hands in a circle. "We're gonna say a prayer for Charlie." As the teammates gathered around, the coach prayed, "Lord, Charlie survived the woods before. And a hurricane. So we believe you're lookin' out for him. Help Charlie and bring him back to Heather."

Gwen grabbed Heather's hand real hard and continued the prayer, "And Lord, we ask that you help Heather. Give her grace to get through these days until she sees Charlie. And help our team stay together."

Many of the girls responded with a soft, "Amen."

Heather was so grateful she didn't know what to say. She just went around and hugged her teammates, and then she said out loud, "You know, I really need to stretch." They all laughed and joined her in stretching exercises.

Practice went well that day and the next, as did the game on Friday. It was a home game, played in a downpour. During most of the game, Heather kept her mind on the field. But every now and again it would drift away to the Francis Marion Woods, where she would envision Charlie sitting under a pine tree shivering in the rain. She felt so sad for him and so angry at that redneck. She had to force her mind back to the game and direct her energies, even her anger, toward the game. At one point, she had so much anger building up in her, that when she got the ball, she drilled a shot from 40 yards out, not caring where it would go. The shot was a rocket that went straight into the upper right hand corner of the goal, beyond the reach of the diving keeper. She hadn't intended it, but it happened. And it was the game-winning goal. The victory assured them of first or second seed in the state tournament. Heather was relieved that they only had one more game to play and that all they had to do was tie in order to get the first seed. Even if they lost, they would get the second seed.

The weekend came and with it a determined plan to search the Francis Marion woods. Heather's mom had hired a special kind of detective to join them. He amusingly called himself "Al the Gator Hunter." Actually, he was an animal tracker, whose name was Al Hunter. He had a bloodhound and all sorts of navigational equipment. When they got to the site where Duke was killed, the bloodhound got on the trail of a dog, but it was not Charlie. He was trailing a golden lab who had passed that way the day before. This trail took them to the town of Honey Hill, whereas Charlie had carefully avoided any contact with human beings. He did not want to get caught like he did before. Any smell of human existence sent him back into the woods. He lived off moles, grass, one duck he caught, and any water he could find along the way. Since it had rained recently, he had enough water. His instincts kept guiding him the way back to Highway 17, where he knew he could then begin his trek back home. But he had to go slowly and cautiously, so as to avoid all contact with humans.

After a long day of hiking, Al's bloodhound had not led them to Charlie. Heather was angry and frustrated, but she kept it inside, trying to keep hope alive. The day ended without finding Charlie. When they got back home late that evening, Dr. Thomson greeted his wife and Heather and then shared with them some grim news. "The sheriff's office called. They said the man who was killed was in fact Duke. Full name was Duke Jackson. And they say he was killed by having his jugular vein sliced—perhaps by an animal. Well, almost certainly by an animal. And probably a dog. They suspect Charlie."

"Good!" Heather blurted out. "He had it comin'. I'm glad Charlie killed him!"

"Well, the problem is, the sheriff's office is bound by law to put Charlie down if they think he killed the man."

Heather jumped up from her chair, grabbed a lamp, and threw it to the floor. "No one on earth is putting Charlie down! You hear me? All those sheriffs are redneck jerks. No one's putting Charlie down! Dad, you can't let them do that! If you don't stop them, I will. When I find Charlie, I'll take him to another state! Another country!"

"Now come on, honey," her dad said. "You know I'm not gonna let anything happen to Charlie. I'll defend him. I'll hire the best lawyer."

The next day, a Sunday, was the first day of November. There was a chill in the morning air, which slowly got broken by the rising sun. All three of the Thomsons drove down to Francis Marion woods, this time without Al Hunter, who had told them that "Sundays are for Jesus and fishin'." Mrs. Thomson had a hunch that Charlie might go back to the same place where she first found him—just north of

Awendaw along Highway 17. If so, then Charlie would be working his way through the woods from the west towards that point. Mrs. Thomson was right. That was exactly what Charlie was doing. But he had to do it in zigzag fashion, whereas they thought he would make a straight beeline down a road called 217. All day they searched this preconceived route; all day they called out his name. At one point in the early afternoon, they heard a dog bark and even saw it run through the woods. It was a golden retriever, but a big one—at least 20 pounds heavier than Charlie.

During the very late afternoon as day turned to dusk, Charlie thought he heard Heather calling his name. He stopped, cocked his head this way and that, perked up his ears, and strained to hear her voice. He was certain it was her voice. So he ran toward her with all his might. He reached road 217 about 10 minutes later, but Heather was not there. All Charlie could see was a car moving off in the distance, growing smaller and smaller in the dim light of dusk turning into dark.

Charlie returned to the woods. The Thomsons went home.

Heather couldn't sleep that night, nor could Charlie. She walked out to her backyard, climbed a tree, and started calling out to him. Not with words. But with her spirit. She called and called until his spirit replied. Charlie spoke to her, "I'm coming." And Heather spoke to him, "I'm coming." They connected—soul to soul, spirit to spirit— as on that first day at the beach. Heather went back to her room and slept. Charlie found a nest of pine needles and slept.

Heather so badly wanted to skip school that day and go to look for Charlie once again. But she had to go with her soccer team to play a game in Charleston that evening. It was the final game of the season, and she had promised everyone that she would play. Her plan was to skip school the next day and the next and the next, if she had to, until she found him.

All the players got on the bus around four, then headed down south to Charleston. Heather sat with her friend Gwen all the way down to McClellanville. Then Heather's coach called her over to sit with her for the rest of the way, so she could discuss strategy.

Heather's mind, however, was on Charlie, not on soccer—especially as they neared Awendaw. Suddenly, Heather's heart started to pound uncontrollably. She started to sweat, and tingles raced up and down her spine. She strongly sensed Charlie's spirit. He was close, real close. She yelled out, "Stop the bus! Stop the bus!" But the driver didn't stop. Then she stood up and screamed at the top of her lungs, "Stop the bus!" The driver, thinking it was an emergency, complied by pulling the bus over to the berm and stopping it. Everyone feared that Heather was having a nervous breakdown as she got up and moved toward the front of the bus. The coach tried to hold her. But she couldn't. Heather ran to the front of the bus, opened the door, and ran toward the woods, calling, "Charlie! Charlie! Charlie!" The coach got out of the bus and tried to pull Heather back in. But Heather pushed her away and called even louder, "Charlie, Charlie! It's me! It's me!" Heather stood there with her arms wide open, calling out his name, as if she were some sort of crazed person or inspired prophet.

Her coach said, "You've got to get back in the bus. We'll be late for the game."

All the other players told her the same. But Gwen spoke up for her, "Give her a few more minutes, will ya? Can't ya see her pain?"

Heather kept calling and calling until he appeared. At first he moved cautiously out of the pinewoods just beyond the berm; then he broke into a full run and came to Heather's arms, who swept him up into a full embrace. The whole team, awed by the moment, broke out into applause and cheers, while Heather cried.

Charlie was back again.

Chapter Nineteen

Fugitive

Heather was in no shape to play a soccer game. She asked to be excused, at least for the first half while she tended to Charlie and got him into the care of her parents who were coming to the game. When the Thomsons arrived and heard that Heather had found Charlie, they were beside themselves with joy and relief. All three of them hugged each other and hugged Charlie. They cried and cried some more. And then they laughed. To see Charlie in the flesh was a miracle.

Dr. Thomson could tell that Charlie was badly undernourished and needed antibiotics for his previous wound that had opened up again. In addition, he had new bruises on his cheek, and lash marks all across his back. He told Heather, "I'm gonna take him to the vet, Dr. Carmichael, and then take him right home."

"No, Dad. I can't let him out of my sight."

"Honey, he needs care. And he needs it now. I've got Dr. Carmichael's cell phone number. He's not far away."

"No, Dad. I can't let him out of my sight. Don't you understand?" she said, as she knelt next to Charlie, hugging him.

"Okay. I tell you what. I'll ask Carmichael to come here. And if he won't, I'll run to the nearest pharmacy and get the necessary stuff until I can take him to a vet tomorrow. I'll also go to grocery store and get him some food."

Heather and Mrs. Thompson stayed with Charlie while Dr. Thomson went to get the things. Once he returned, Heather felt good enough and calm enough to rejoin her team. It was nearly halftime and the score was 1-1. Sandra, the other forward, had made an awesome goal. Heather stretched during halftime, apologized to her coach for pushing her, and thanked the team for their support. The coach told Heather that she would play her in the last 20 minutes. "Heather, just watch the game for awhile. Get your mind and body focused, and then I'll put you in."

"Fine, coach. Whatever's best for the team."

The first 20 minutes went by, and the coach called for a substitution. But neither of the forwards came out. Instead, the coach called out the central defender, otherwise known as the stopper. She had been limping for the past two minutes. "Heather, we're playing for a tie. Don't let anything get near our box. Understand?"

"Got it, coach," she said with a smile.

"Keep it in their half for the next 20 minutes," she yelled out after Heather, who ran out onto the field with incredible energy. For the rest of the game, she stopped everything up the middle and even helped defend the attack on the sides. And then she made superb passes to the two forwards, one of whom scored a goal with two minutes left to go in the game. Their team had won, and they got first seed in the championship tournament.

As Heather ran around congratulating her teammates after the game, her coach came up and hugged her, saying, "Think we found another position for ya, girl."

"Cool, coach. Whatever's best for the team. I'm just glad Charlie's back."

Heather rejoined her parents and Charlie. And the four of them drove home as a happy family once again. Charlie lay on the back seat, with his head on Heather's lap, who stroked his soft furry head again and again, telling him over and over, "I'm sorry I left you. I'm so sorry."

Heather's mom then spoke up. "I asked the hospital to give me my two week vacation early, and the request was granted. I did it so I could look for Charlie. Now that we've found him, I want to take the two weeks to be with him. That way, Heather, you can go to school everyday, and stay with soccer for the next two weeks, until the championships are over. You won't have to worry. I will watch him like a hawk."

"Oh, Mom. Thanks. What a relief," Heather replied.

The next day, after Heather went to school, Dr. Thomson took Charlie to a local vet to have his wound stitched. Heather knew this was going to happen, so nothing was being done without her knowledge. Mrs. Thompson stayed home to catch up on some housework. It wasn't 15 minutes after her husband left with Charlie that the doorbell rang and she opened the door to the sight of two policemen.

"Ma'am, are you Mrs. Thomson?"

"Yes."

"We're sorry, but we have a court order to pick up your dog."

Everything her husband told her a few days before flashed through her mind. She knew that they were going to kill Charlie for having attacked Duke. So she collected her thoughts for a moment and said calmly, "Our dog ran away."

"But word is you found him."

"Well, you can search the house and premises and see that there's no dog here."

At that, the policemen entered the house, walked through it, and then went out into the backyard. As soon as they stepped outside, Mrs. Thomson called her husband on his cell phone. "Paul, the cops are here to take away Charlie. They're in the backyard. Take Charlie and drive him north. Then call me later. I'll come get him. Do it now!"

After a few minutes, the officers returned and one of them said, "Well, there ain't no dog here right now. But there sure was one."

"Yea, there sure was," Mrs. Thomson replied, who then showed them out the front door.

A half hour later, the phone rang. It was Dr. Thomson, who was with Charlie in Murrels Inlet up the road a bit. "I have to get to work, Jenny. I'm very late as is."

"I know. I know. I've packed, and I've called my sister in Columbus. I'll be taking Charlie there. You can work out the legal stuff while I'm gone. I'm stopping by the school to tell Heather, then I'll meet you."

When Mrs. Thomson got to the school, they called Heather out of class. Her mother then asked her to come out into the parking lot and get in the car. When Mrs. Thomson explained what had happened and what her plan was, Heather protested. Then her mother took her hands in hers, looked her straight in the eyes and said, "I love you. And I know how much you love Charlie. I'm doing this because I love you and because we all love Charlie."

"But, Mom, I want to be with him. I'm going to come with you."

"No you're not. You're going to do your part in life right now. And I'm gonna keep Charlie alive. Then we will reunite. And that's it."

Heather understood. She knew that her mom was right, even though it would break her heart yet again to be without him. They kissed goodbye and Mrs. Thomson promised that she would take care of Charlie like her own child.

Chapter Twenty

Charlie's Trial

The police came to the Thomsons' house two more times in the next week, trying to fulfill the court order. On the second try, Dr. Thomson informed them, "I've had hired a lawyer to reverse the court order, so this will no longer be an issue."

One of them replied, "Sir, until that happens, we're fixin' to get that dog."

"Good luck," Dr. Thomson said curtly.

The two walked back to their patrol car, as Heather pulled up in her VW bug. She got out immediately, slammed the door, went right up to them, and demanded, "And just what are ya'll doin' here?"

"We're here to fulfill a court order," one of them said wryly.

"And just what is that court order?"

"To take away your dog."

"And what do you mean by 'take away your dog'?" Heather demanded even more fervently.

"You know"—and then the officer made the gesture of cutting his throat.

It was all Heather could do to keep herself from grabbing him by the throat and strangling him to death. But she restrained her fists and walked away without a further word. When she went inside, she flew into a rage. Her father could scarcely control her.

"Heather, I've got a lawyer who's making an appeal to the magistrate to reverse the court order. He's a top Charleston lawyer, well-respected around here. That's all we can do right now. You've got to get control of yourself."

Heather reluctantly agreed, but it took her about an hour to calm down. She listened to her favorite music, the Alman Brothers, then called her mom on the phone to talk to her and then to Charlie. Her mom was at her sister's place in Columbus, her old hometown, and assured her that she was taking excellent care of Charlie. She held the phone up to Charlie's ear so he could hear Heather tell him, "You're the best, Charlie. The absolute best. I miss you."

During the next few days, Heather's team started the state tournament. As the first seed, they played weaker teams for the first two matches and easily won. Heather played forward for half the game, and central defender for the other half. The coach could tell that her thoughts weren't completely in the game, but still Heather was an excellent player even at 80%. Gwen kept her pumped up, especially when Heather played defense—because the two could talk to each other.

At the end of the week, her dad told her that a trial had been set for the following Wednesday. It would be a half-day trial, with a six-person jury. The prosecuting lawyer would be working for the county on behalf of a police order to dispose of a dog that was allegedly charged with killing a man. Since a dog cannot defend itself, the burden fell on Mr. James Radcliffe, an attorney from Charleston. An owner of golden retrievers all his life, he took a personal interest in the case.

They spent Saturday morning at the lawyer's office to go through everything. Mr. Radcliffe, a sharp lawyer in his mid-fifties, was confident he could win the case on two counts: (1) there was no proof that Charlie severed the man's jugular veins, only that some animal—"presumably a canine" (as the autopsy report stated)—had done so; (2) even if it was Charlie, he was acting in self-defense because the bruises on his face and back side were new wounds inflicted by hitting and whipping. The veterinarian report affirmed this. But Mr. Radcliffe didn't think he would even have to go to the second point. He'd win it on the first. Then Mr. Radcliffe told

Heather that she would have to testify about Duke's two attempts to murder her. He added, "The other attorney will try to throw out your testimony. But I will argue that it establishes character."

News got out about Charlie's trial. Everybody in the high school heard about it. The magistrate's court room was not big enough to hold more than 40 people. So a lot of people waited outside, which attracted the attention of the local press. The prosecuting attorney, a bowlegged, beer-bellied 50-year-old man named Clyde Hancock, made a motion that the trial be postponed until the dog was in custody. Mr. Radcliffe objected, stating, "The dog is not on trial. This case is about reversing a court order. The dog does not need to be here."

The magistrate agreed with Mr. Radcliffe, who then presented a host of witnesses. He called Shelby Stanton to the stand. He was at Taco Bell and witnessed Duke trying to run over Heather. Shelby said, "She was runnin' after her dog that man snatched from her car. He looked behind him, saw her comin', gunned the engine, and clean knocked her over."

He called the police officers to the stand who saw Heather's car riddled with shotgun holes that had come from Duke's rifle. One of them said, "Sure enough, that man was fixin' to kill that girl."

He called Pete Welton, a co-worker of Duke's, who testified, "Duke talked 'bout nothin' else but layin' his hands on that $10,000 reward. I told him to give it up. Wouldn't listen."

Another person named Slim Johnson, a neighbor of Duke's, took the stand and said, "That ol' boy sure was mean to his dogs. Whipped 'em, kicked 'em somethin' fierce."

Then he called Heather to the stand, who told the whole story of how Duke snatched Charlie from her car; then just about killed her when she tried to get Charlie back.

The prosecuting attorney couldn't controvert anyone's testimony or even make them look foolish. He chose not to question Heather because he could tell that she had the sympathy of the jury. His sole witness was the doctor who performed the autopsy on Duke Jackson, who had written in his report that "the severing of the victim's jugular vein may have been caused by the piercing of an animal, perhaps a canine."

In his cross-examination, Mr. Radcliffe ripped this testimony to pieces. He did it masterfully, like a dog chewing off every morsel of meat from a bone. First, he picked apart the doctor's ability to differentiate between a canine bite and a wolf bite. Mr. Radcliffe asked him, "Have you ever seen a wolf bite?"

"No."

"Do you think there are wolves in the Francis Marion woods?"

"I reckon."

"You reckoned right. Furthermore, have you ever seen the bite marks of a golden retriever?"

"No, but I've seen the bite marks of a German shepherd."

"Oh, but golden retrievers aren't German shepherds, are they?"

"No."

Then Mr. Radcliffe called up the officer who first saw Duke's corpse and asked him what he saw. "Well, I saw a mangled corpse that was hardly even human any more—it had been so gouged by vultures."

"And don't you suppose by other wild animals, as well?"

"Well, sure."

Then he asked the officer, "Did you collect any forensic evidence from the scene? Any saliva? Any samples of blood?"

"No."

"And what happened to Duke's body after the autopsy?"

"He was immediately cremated."

Mr. Radcliffe had no further questions.

In his closing arguments, the prosecuting attorney tried to get the jury not to be sympathetic to Heather, for that was a different issue. He tried to get them to see that a dog had attacked a man and killed him—and that dog must have been Charlie. Therefore, Charlie was a threat to society and must be put away. These final words evoked audible objection from the crowd, whereupon the magistrate ordered them to silence.

Mr. Radcliffe's closing arguments were straightforward and compelling. He pointed to the witnesses who saw Duke's brutal behavior and then he affirmed that Charlie was a normal golden retriever, the breed of which has never been known to attack human beings. Upon making this affirmation, he cited some very impressive statistics. In his closing words, he stated, "We do not know who or what killed Duke Jackson. But we can be certain that it wasn't Charlie. There is absolutely no evidence to prove this. I ask you, the jury, to overturn the court order that says this dog must be put away—that is, euthanized. And I ask the court to issue a new order that would protect this animal from any further harm."

The jury exited the courtroom into a small jury room and returned with their verdict in less the time that it takes to drink a cup of lemonade on a hot summer's day. The main juror rose to his feet and said, "We, the jury, overturn the court order."

The magistrate affirmed their verdict, but he denied Mr. Radcliffe's request for an order of protection, saying, "You know very well that such orders can only be applied to people. Nice try." The two winked at each other, and shook hands, while the audience in the courtroom burst into applause.

Heather and her dad hugged each other, then hugged Mr. Radcliffe, who was gloating in his swift victory. As the courtroom emptied, a reporter from the local paper approached Heather and asked her for an interview and a picture of Charlie. Her father intervened, "We'll be happy to give you a picture of Charlie tomorrow, but the interview will have to wait a bit."

"Why?" the reporter asked.

"We'll tell you later."

Heather and her dad got in their car, and started driving home. Heather picked up her dad's cell phone, called her mom, and bellowed out the entire story. She was ecstatic. Her dad was ecstatic. And so was her mom. She and Charlie would come home tomorrow.

Chapter Twenty-one

Missing Him

All the next day Heather's mind was not on school and even not on the soccer game coming up that night. All she could think of was Charlie and having him back. You see, Charlie wasn't a pet. He was an awesome soul in a dog's body. He brought joy to everyone. His smile was radiant; he caused everyone around him to smile, especially Heather. He was a gift from heaven to those on earth. Heather really missed him, missed that smile, that joy that emanated from his being. No one else on earth gave that joy to her in that way.

Even though Charlie had gone through so many sufferings, he was not bitter. He still had joy and it always glowed, sometimes soft and serene like a candle at night; other times, bold and burning like the noonday sun. Various people, here and there, caught a glimpse of that radiant joy. Heather was blessed to have it continually. She had really missed his sweet companionship.

That night was the fourth game in their state championship matches. If they won, they would get to go to the finals. Heather tried to put her heart and mind into the game, but it was tough. She really hoped her mom and Charlie would arrive before the game started, but they didn't. Just before game time, Mrs. Thomson called her husband on his cell phone and told him that she was 30 minutes away from the school. Dr. Thomson then related the message to Heather as she was stretching on the sideline. "Honey, Mom's a half-hour away. You'll see Charlie at halftime, if it's okay with the coach."

A huge smile beamed across her face. She ran over to the coach and told her the news, begging her to see Charlie at halftime. "Okay," coach said, "but only for five minutes."

"Yes!" Heather said, making a gesture with her hands as if she had just scored a goal.

"Now go out there and get some goals for us! I'm playing you up front the entire game. Sandra's not at full speed because of her hamstring. You've got to make runs and you've got to be shootin'."

"Yes, ma'am," she responded with confidence.

The exciting anticipation of seeing Charlie pumped her up. Heather was as high as a pelican soaring over the ocean. She took the field with verve, lots of chatter, and spring in her legs. When the ball came to Heather or even near her, she was on it, dribbling, distributing, and taking a few shots when the opportunity came. The keeper for the other team (from Columbia) was quick and agile; she stopped every shot. Gwen was also on her game; she stopped every shot from the opponents. With one minute to go before halftime, the score was 0-0. Heather had been fouled just outside the box. The coach yelled out for her to take the free kick. As she got up from the ground and turned around to see if the coach had any further instructions, she saw her mom and Charlie on the other side of fence walking up toward the field. She wanted to stop and yell out to them, but, instead, she got control of herself and focused on the kick. She stalled for time by placing the ball in just the right spot and asking the referee to make sure the human wall of the defending team was 10 yards back. As the referee paced off the distance, she looked back and saw that Charlie was looking straight at her. Then she turned her head toward goal, lowered it, took aim, made two steps into the ball, and rocketed a shot into the upper right hand corner of the goal past the outstretched arms of the keeper. As the ball went into the net, making that swoosh sound all strikers love to hear, Heather yelled out, "That's for Charlie!" All her teammates came around her and hugged her, as the referee blew the whistle for halftime.

Heather ran over to the fence and jumped it. She got down on her knees and threw her arms around Charlie, who licked her face streaming with tears. "Oh, Charlie, it's sooooooo good to have you back. No one's ever going to take you away again. You stay here with Mom. I'll be back when the game's over."

Charlie wanted to run after her, but Mrs. Thomson restrained him with the leash. She, too, got down on her knees next to Charlie and said, "Stay here, boy. We'll watch the game from here."

Then Dr. Thomson came over. He hugged his wife and kissed her, telling her how much he missed her. Then he hugged Charlie and said, "I missed you, guy." Charlie licked his face and barked once, which was all the communication any person could ask for. Charlie missed him, too.

The three stood behind the fence and watched the rest of the game. Dr. Thomson went on and on about the trial and how suave and sagacious Mr. Radcliffe was. He thanked his wife profusely for taking Charlie away, and told them both yet again how delighted he was to have them back. They could see the delight in Heather who raced around the field like a gazelle—with her long legs reaching for the ball, dribbling it, and passing. She had only one more shot on goal, which the keeper saved. Gwen was the real hero of the second half. With 10 minutes left to go in the game, the team from Columbia got a corner kick. When the ball swerved in toward the goal, a player headed it in toward the goal. Gwen leaped to her left and just managed to deflect the ball away with her finger tips. Columbia got another corner kick. Again, when the ball swerved in toward the goal, a player got her foot to it and made a volley that looked like a sure goal. The home team crowd gasped, but Gwen came through again. She leaped to her right and punched the ball away, which one of her defenders then cleared by booting it down field. By this time in the game, all of the home team was backed up in a defensive position. Columbia had one minute left to make a final push. They got the ball in the box, and one of their players was just about to make a quick cut and then take a shot, when her legs were taken out from underneath her by a defender. Columbia was awarded a penalty kick.

As the kicker lined up to take the shot, Gwen waited on her goal line on her toes. As the kicker advanced toward the ball, Gwen took two quick steps forward then dove to the right, knocking away the ball with her right hand. Heather had run in with the shot, and was there to clear the ball from any further danger. Twenty seconds later, the referee blew the whistle to end the game. Everyone on the team ran up and hugged Gwen. Then the home crowd started pouring onto the field. In her excitement, Mrs. Thomson let go of Charlie's leash. He jumped the fence and ran to the girls, who included him in their dancing circle of joy. He leaped, barked, and spun in circles.

Chapter Twenty-two

The Championship Game

The whole school was "all abuzz" about the big game coming up. Girls and guys were giving Heather hi-fives before school, between classes, and after school. Many of them, who normally don't go to soccer games, saw her goal in the last game and were awed by her power and accuracy. All week long the comment was, "Hope you win state!" To tell you the truth, Heather didn't care that much about winning the state championship. She had Charlie back and that was all that mattered. Nevertheless, her teammates, especially Gwen, kept her pumped up. As always, she asked Heather to stay 10 more minutes after practice to do penalty kicks. It had really paid off in the last game, so Heather obliged her, even though she wanted to get home and see Charlie.

She knew that it had been a long day for Charlie, even though her parents had hired a retired man to stay with Charlie during the day while all the family members were away. Because of Charlie's recent notoriety, the family was concerned that some "nutcase" would try to steal him or do him harm. This retiree, named James Long, had worked with a canine unit in the police force in Columbus, Ohio, before he moved to South Carolina, after the death of his wife. The Thomsons had known him for years because he had previously lived in the same neighborhood. He loved dogs, and he quickly grew to love Charlie.

No matter who got close to Charlie—and he usually let people do this, unless they were evil—no one was as close to him as Heather.

The two shared the same room, even the same queen-sized bed. While Heather studied or talked on the phone (which she always did stretched out on her bed), Charlie was at her side or at her feet, enjoying a tummy rub.

For the first few weeks after Charlie's return, James Long accompanied Heather and Charlie on their early morning walks along the beach—just for extra protection. Charlie's wounds had almost completely healed, so he was able to run at full pace. Like the wind. Like a gazelle. Graceful. Swift. A pure joy to observe: his nostrils flared in the sea breeze; the feathering on his chest and legs and tail sailing in the wind; the graceful curves of his occiput, crest, and withers swaying in the run; his four legs galloping in rhythm through the shallows; his flews flapping; eyes widening; and whole joyous body brimming over like an ocean full of fish. He chased everything. Seagulls, sandpipers, pelicans, ghost crabs, minnows, mullets, and bluefish. Most of all, he chased life. He could never get enough of it. There was never enough life for Charlie. He was too big for it, too beyond it. Heather knew this, because he took her there sometimes. He took her beyond her problems, her self, her world. With Charlie, she was not ugly. She was not too tall. She was not just a jock. She was alive.

The week passed quickly. Friday came, and with it the championship game. Since Heather's team was first seed, the game was going to be at home. Heather's parents promised that they would bring Charlie to the game, and they would watch from behind the end zone fence. Heather thanked them for this and for all that they had done for Charlie. James Long also decided to come along, just to give extra support.

The team entered into the game prepared and confident. Their defense had been stalwart recently. They needed to keep up a strong defense, and the offense needed to step it up a notch. The other forward, Sandra, would be able to play only the last 15 minutes of the game because of her hamstring injury. So they were counting on the midfield to bring the ball forward and feed it to Heather, who would be the lone striker. The other team, from Spartanburg, had the best record in the state for goals scored. They had a powerful offense and very strong defense. So Heather's coach explained to the team that she would be satisfied with a 1-0 win.

True to the coach's prediction, it was a defensive match for most of the first half. But then things changed that night under a full moon and under the lights of that stadium. Late in the first half Spartanburg got a free kick from 20 yards out. The ball took a weird deflection off the human wall of defenders, fooled Gwen, and went in for the first goal. At the beginning of the second half, a ball was kicked by a Spartanburg striker that hit another player and bounced up into the hand of a defender. Wrongly, the referee awarded a penalty kick. (A true penalty happens when a player purposely plays a ball with her hand in the penalty area.) The fans, outraged, went nuts. Heather's coach flew into a rage, stormed out onto the field, and started shouting at the referee. She was immediately given a red card and thrown out of the game. Gwen also flipped out, but the referee gave her a yellow card and told her to calm down. She calmed down enough to get ready for the penalty kick. But the kicker was too good. Spartanburg was up 2-0.

Five minutes later, Spartanburg scored again off a corner kick. With the score 3-0 against them, and the head coach out of the game, the assistant coach decided to put three forwards up front. The decision paid off. Even though Spartanburg was packed into a defensive shell, Heather and the other forwards found ways around them, especially by doing one-touch soccer—quick, short passes to players weaving and moving into space. Heather and another girl named Maria connected on the first goal, and the crowd went wild. Fifteen minutes later the same duo were just about to connect on another goal when Heather was tripped by a defender. She was awarded a penalty kick. Her nerves were getting the best of her. So she turned around, looked for Charlie, and saw him as calm as ever. She gathered her strength and mind. She stepped up to the ball, 12 yards from the goal, and struck it into the lower lefthand corner of the goal for the second goal.

There was only seven minutes left in the half. The home team needed to score in order to tie so as to send the game into overtime.

They found the will and the way to do just that. With one minute left, the referee (in return for his bad call before) awarded them a free kick just outside the box. The team asked Heather to take it. So she again gathered all her strength and will, and tried to tune out the crowd that was now chanting her name. She readjusted the position of the ball and asked the referee to make sure the human wall of defenders was 10 yards back. She looked over at Charlie and her parents, saw their calm, and took aim. As before, she delivered a rocket—a shot straight into the upper right hand corner of the goal. Her team was elated. The fans went crazy. Heather's parents jumped for joy, and Charlie spun in circles.

Both teams drank as much as they could before going into overtime. They stretched, worked out some cramps, and got their heads ready for two five-minute overtime periods. Whichever team scored first in overtime was the automatic winner. It's called "the golden goal." If no one scored, it would go into a shootout. No soccer player wants to go into a shootout because it is so nerve-racking and because it really doesn't indicate who the best team is.

The first five minute overtime period was a defensive battle. Neither team committed players forward, and the forwards on each team were just plain tired. As they began the second overtime period, Heather was really tiring. After a long run that ended in a goal kick situation for the other team, she stood about 20 yards out from the goal. Normally, she would have backed up several more yards to get into proper position for a goal kick, but since she was struggling to get more air, she stood there gasping. The goalkeeper for Spartanburg lined up to take the goal kick. She stepped up to the ball and slipped as she took the kick, and the ball shanked off her foot right to the feet of Heather who easily—and almost unconsciously—kicked the ball into the empty net.

All of a sudden, the opposing team members all around her fell to the ground. Heather didn't know what to feel. Empathy for the keeper? Glad the game was over? At the same time, the crowd started cheering hysterically. The band blasted the school theme song, and Heather's teammates swarmed her. She didn't feel deserving. She just felt relieved.

Her coach came down from the stands and ran out to congratulate the team. Heather was swarmed for nearly 10 minutes—by fans, by players, and by her parents. Eventually she found her way to Charlie and Charlie to her. In a team picture taken at the end of these celebrations, Heather was on her knees next to Charlie hugging him.

Chapter Twenty-three

Rest and Relaxation

With soccer season done and the holidays coming up—Thanksgiving, Christmas, and New Year—Heather found a chance to relax, reflect, and enjoy some peace. Autumn had been quite the tumultuous season. A hurricane, Charlie stolen, a court trial, a championship soccer season. Heather could tell that her parents also needed some "om" time, as did Charlie. Her mom put it well when she said, "I'm asking God for an uneventful holiday season."

Heather and Charlie still took walks on the beach in late November and December. Heather saw some of the guys put on their wet suits to go surf the cold ocean waters. She wasn't into that. Her season, she figured, was from late April to late October. Charlie was different. He liked to go into the waters even in December. So Heather would pitch sticks into the sea for him to fetch. One of Heather's favorite things to do on her walks was to look for the bottle-nosed dolphins. Whenever she saw a pod of them swimming by, about 75 to 100 yards out, she would walk real fast on the beach, staying parallel with them. Sometimes they would move in closer and put on spectacular shows. They would leap and flip and swirl. They would flap their tails on the sea's surface, making booming sounds. This behavior signaled to other dolphins that it was time for feeding. The pod would keep circling the smaller fish, blowing bubbles to ensnare them in a makeshift trap, then move in, one after the other, to take turns feeding until the wide circle of smaller fish (usually bluefish or spot) got smaller and smaller.

When the dolphins moved in close—about 30 to 40 yards out from the beach—Charlie could see the activity. Not being able to resist the excitement of wild life, he would plunge in and swim toward the circle. Heather feared he'd get bit or something—or that a shark would come. But that never happened. In fact, Charlie rarely ever got too close to this migrating circle as it meandered around in the ocean, even though he swam after it for all he was worth.

Charlie had a routine when he came home from his swims at the beach. He would dive into Heather's bed, roll around in her blankets, put his nose under every blanket, then spin to his back, drying off his back on her blankets. Then he would jump off her bed and shake and shake. Heather always laughed during this routine, even though it meant that she would have to take all her blankets outside to shake them and then hang them out to dry.

Charlie had something else he really like to do: visit a female golden retriever, named Sis, who lived across the street. The owner, Mr. Rand, really liked Charlie's coloring. He wasn't pure golden; he had a tint of red running through his blond hair. And the man liked his physique. Even though he was small, Charlie was starting to fill out a bit. Mr. Rand hoped the two would mate. Charlie had not been neutered when the Thomsons found him. They had intended to do it, but Charlie had been through so many traumas they didn't want to put him through yet another one. As for Charlie, he was glad he still had his manhood. Within weeks, he impregnated Sis.

The puppies came two months later in late January, and the third in the litter looked just like Charlie. He was a male named Spin at birth because he spun out of his mother's womb. Five days later, Heather found out about the births. When Heather saw Spin she fell in love with him and wanted to keep him. But Mr. Rand had already pre-sold all four puppies to various people for $700 each. He had been laid off from work and really needed the money, so he wouldn't give Spin to Heather, who had thought he would give her one of the puppies since Charlie was the father.

"Sorry," Mr. Rand said. "I never promised you a puppy. And even if you had the money, other people picked Spin out a day after his birth."

Heather was crushed and dumbfounded. She wanted to cuss the man out. Instead, she said, "So it was all a business to you? Letting Charlie be with Sis? Well, he's not comin' over anymore! You ol'—" Then she bit her lower lip and exited his house, slamming the door behind her.

Heather's mom, Jenny, was sympathetic. She also assumed that Mr. Rand would offer them a puppy, although she hadn't thought it through if she really wanted one. As they talked, Charlie came into the kitchen, sat beside Heather, and put his paw up for a handshake. "Charlie," she said, "I guess I don't really want to share you with another dog, even though he is your son. You should see your pups!"

"Mom, do you think Charlie can see his pups?"

"You just told me that you would never take Charlie there again!"

"I know, you're right. I was pretty ticked off that old bald buzzard."

"Honey. You shouldn't talk that way about people."

"But what if it's true?"

"Well, he is bald. And he is old. But he's not a buzzard."

The two enjoyed a good laugh, then prepared dinner for dad. When he got home, he got an earful from both the women in his life. He also assumed that Mr. Rand would have offered them a puppy, but understood that there was no obligation to do so. When he telephoned Mr. Rand and asked him to reconsider, Mr. Rand replied, "My hands are tied. I've taken the money already, and another little girl has already picked out Spin as her own. In fact, she and her father are here right now looking at him."

"Who are they?"

"The Plymouth family who lives down the street."

Dr. Thomson relayed to his wife and Heather the words of Mr. Rand, and then Dr. Thomson said, "It's just as well. I think Charlie and Charlie alone should get all our attention."

And he did.

As winter went into spring (which happens at the end of February in South Carolina) and spring went into summer, Heather enjoyed hundreds of wonderful beach mornings with Charlie. She surfed when there was surf, and ran or swam with Charlie when there wasn't. Gwen joined them sometimes. As always, all the guys would look at Gwen, more beautiful than ever. Heather was sure that some of them must have wondered why she hung out with such a geek like her. One day after Heather left the beach and Gwen was getting ready to go, a guy actually asked her, "How come you hang out with that geek?"

"'Cause she's got a beautiful soul. And your comment shows you don't."

Gwen was a spiritual person. She loved Jesus, but didn't talk about it much to other people, even Heather. Gwen figured that Heather would one day find Jesus to be real. Heather knew that Gwen was a Christian and that she herself wasn't. But she liked having the company of someone with a clean mind and cheerful spirit. So the two kept being friends that summer and into the fall, which would bring Gwen's senior year and Heather's junior year. It would also bring soccer and possibly hurricanes. Heather wanted to be ready for both.

Chapter Twenty-four

Bad News

The Thomsons came up with a plan if there was a hurricane warning, which is usually signaled a day or two in advance. If it happened again, Heather would not even go to school. Rather, the whole family, with Charlie, would go to the home of a co-worker and friend of Dr. Thomson's. This man, named Dr. Colman, was very hospitable. He owned a large home in the country near Andrews, 30 miles inland. They would be safe there.

True to form, the weather patterns lined up just right at the end of September for another hurricane. This one was mammoth, predicted to be at least a level four. The forecasters were predicting a direct hit on Charleston or just north, which meant that they would get some severe weather in Andrews, while gale force winds would hit the coast.

Hurricanes are awful and awesome things. You can't think God's behind them, but people sure pray to God when they come. This one named Lucy came like a demon out of hell. It's funny, how they give hurricanes names. But it's true. Each hurricane has a mind of its own. No matter what is predicted, the winds will go where they want to go. Certain houses will be flattened; others left alone. Some people will drown; most are smart enough to seek higher ground.

Lucy brought powerful winds with her, over 110 miles an hour, and a huge downpour of water. The eye of the storm went over Myrtle Beach, 25 miles north of the Thomsons' home in Pawleys

Island. This meant that their home didn't get a direct hit, but close to it. The Thomsons themselves made it through fine because they were 30 miles inland, staying in a sturdy home when the winds and rain hit. But it was a different story for their own house and property. Many pines were snapped and their entire roof was taken off, creating a disaster inside their home. Added to this, flood waters reached such a level that water streamed into their house about three inches high. When the hurricane had passed and the roads opened up, they returned to see the disaster. As they drove down their street and got close to their house, Mrs. Thomson cried. Dr. Thompson audibly moaned. Heather was sad. Charlie jumped out of the car and ran around the yard in foot-deep water.

"Don't worry, honey," he told his wife. "Insurance will take care of it, even a place for us to rent while this is being fixed."

"I wish we were back in Ohio," she complained. "Why did we ever move here? There's been nothin' but troubles. With rednecks, with Southerners who can't stand Yankees, and with hurricanes! I wanna go back to Ohio."

"Well, ya'll can go back, but Charlie and I are stayin' here," Heather remarked. "I'm going out to start clearing away some trees."

Dr. Thomson spoke to his wife. "I'll take care of everything. I'm calling our insurance company right now. Good thing I have flood insurance. I'll have a roofer here tomorrow. Know a guy who owes me a favor. We can stay at the Ramada tonight and then figure out tomorrow how long the clean up will take." Then he gave Jenny a hug and a kiss, and wiped a tear streaming down her cheek.

"Well, I am glad we're getting rid of these carpets. Can't stand 'em," she said, trying to make some humor.

"How 'bout wood floors?" he asked.

"Really? You mean it?"

"Why not?" he responded with a smile.

Some kindness healed the situation. And the repair work on the house was done in three weeks. In the meantime, soccer started back up again for Heather. The days are still long in September, so she could take Charlie to the beach in the mornings or late afternoons. In late September the ocean water is still warm and the surf is quite good. She and Charlie enjoyed both. She was getting better at surfing, such that she could catch far more waves than before and keep her balance while going down the wave. Charlie was filling out, so he could take longer swims without getting chilled. Now and again, when the waves were manageable, he swam out for a ride on the surfboard.

Heather's soccer team was not as good as the last two years because eight of last year's starting players graduated. The coach knew that this would be a building year. Still, she had Gwen in goal and Heather up front. As the season went on, however, it became clearer that Heather had to play center midfield to control the flow of the game as best as possible. This meant two things: she ran herself into the ground and she had less scoring opportunities. The team was having a 50-50 season by the time they came to the last two weeks. Heather had to play beyond herself for the remaining games. The team barely made it to the playoffs and was eliminated in the first round.

When the season was over, Heather was exhausted to the point of getting really sick. And it was a sickness that led to more sickness and extreme fatigue. She only had energy to make it to school and back again. She would take Charlie to the beach most days and just sit there wrapped in a poncho or blanket, watching Charlie run around. She didn't have the energy—or even the willpower—to walk with him or throw sticks. Besides, the chilling nor'eastern winds would knife right through here if she tried to walk along the water's edge. This lasted for weeks, all the way into the holiday season. She got thinner and thinner, paler and paler, like the waning moon. Her spirit was gone and so was her lust for life.

Her father was quite concerned that she had something wrong with her internally. So he took her to a friend of his who was an internist. This man, named Dr. Carmen, ran many urine and blood tests on Heather and discovered that she was having kidney failure. Further tests revealed that both her kidneys were failing. Heather was aghast when she heard the report. At first, she denied it. Then she had to accept it when the doctor ordered immediate kidney dialysis, and her parents drove her to the kidney dialysis center in Murrels Inlet. She couldn't believe that she, a sixteen-year-old girl, was having kidney failure. All throughout her first treatment, she sat there saying nothing, but her mind was racing with thoughts. She thought of how crazy life was in the preciousness of its shortness, like a Fourth of July fireworks display; like a beautiful wave mounting, forming, peeling, crashing, foaming, fizzling; like a morning on the beach with Charlie—over almost as soon as it began.

She said nothing all the way home nor at dinner. Her parents respected her silence. Besides, they didn't know what to say. They just swallowed their grief and tried to look calm. But everyone's insides were churning like angry waves. Heather went to her room after dinner and flopped down on her bed next to Charlie. The two lay in the silence of their shared existence. Heather thought, *Dogs are so lucky they don't know about death—that they're gonna die. They just live.* Then she said out loud, "Isn't that right, Charlie? You just live, don't you?" Charlie didn't answer. He just flapped his tail on the bed and pushed his muzzle under Heather's arm. As she began to scratch his tummy, she heard a knock on the door. Thinking it was one of her parents, she called out, "Leave me alone! I'm trying to sleep!"

"It's me, Gwen," the voice replied.

"Sorry, Gwen. Come on in."

Gwen came in and sat with Heather for awhile in her bedroom, and then asked her, "Heather, would you like to know Jesus?"

"Sure, Gwen. I wondered how long it was gonna be before you asked."

"Well, there's timin' to these things," she responded with a soft smile.

"Yea. I know. Now's the time," Heather said, holding back some tears.

"Just say to Jesus whatever you want to say. He's alive. He's here. He cares for you and loves you," Gwen told her reassuringly.

Nervous and anxious, apprehensive and excited, Heather held Gwen's hands, took a deep breath, sighed, then said, "Jesus, I want to know you. Help me with my problem. I'm sorry for all the bad things I've thought, but I want to live." As she spoke, Heather was effused with the Spirit of Jesus coming over her like a soft waterfall, coming into her like a sweet liquid, filling up her empty spirit, soothing her soul. She cried and laughed, laughed and cried. Gwen did the same. Then the two hugged, with Charlie sitting right next to them, wagging his tail, flapping it on the bed.

"Do you think Jesus could give me new kidneys?" Heather asked.

"I'd give you mine, if I could," Gwen responded sincerely.

"I know. But you're not a match."

"How do you know?"

"You're not kin."

"But I'm your sister now."

The two smiled and knew it was true.

Chapter Twenty-five

Medicine and Miracle

December is a fickle month is South Carolina. Some days it can be as cold as Ohio in winter and even drop some snow. Other days the sun will pierce the blue sky with penetrating warmth. The next day had both. It snowed in the morning under gray heavy clouds. But the sky broke open bright blue by midday and the sun's rays licked up all the snow. Charlie enjoyed the snow while it lasted, and Heather enjoyed watching him enjoy the snow.

Before nightfall, which comes early in December, Dr. Carmen telephoned Dr. Thomson and told him that he would like to check each family member for a potential kidney donor. In such situations, a family does not have time to go into self-pity or remorse. Survival mode takes over. Courage is what's needed, not cowardice. So everyone was trying to be strong.

Soon each person in the family was tested for a kidney match: Heather's father, mother, and even her older brother James, who had come home for the holidays. Within the week, it was discovered that Heather's mother was the best match. When Mrs. Thomson heard the news, she was elated. Without hesitation, Mrs. Thomson got herself ready to give up one of her kidneys so that Heather could live. Her sacrifice would be sweet and sensible, for a mother has no greater love than for her daughter.

Heather was amazed at her attitude. "Mom, you're not even going to think about it?"

"Are you kiddin'? I already thought about it. I prayed that I would be the match."

"You prayed, Mom?"

"Yea, I asked God for this special favor."

"That's awesome. I also prayed the other day—with Gwen. I asked Jesus to be with me for the rest of my life."

"That's good, dear," Mrs. Thomson said, as she stroked Heather's hair. "I'm sure he will. He'll be with both of us."

The day before the operation, the Thomsons drove down to the beach to give Charlie a chance to run around. Since Heather had been sick for the past month, different people (especially Gwen) had taken turns taking him to the beach. This particular December day was unusually warm, around 70 degrees at midday. Heather got out of the car, gazed out at the serene ocean, soaked in the sun's rays, and silently prayed. Her mother joined her, put her arms around her and hugged her daughter only like a mother can do. Then Dr. Thomson joined in, and even James, who normally would be too macho to join a group hug. But since no one was on the beach to see him do it, he gave his sister and mom a big hug. Charlie squeezed his way into the midst of them, relishing this strange, teary-eyed gathering.

That evening the entire soccer team came over to Heather's house. They gave her a brand-new soccer ball with all their signatures on it

"Thanks, guys, the ball is awesome. The best gift ever."

Then Gwen gave her a gift, a black leather Bible. Heather opened it, smelled the leather, turned the crisp thin pages, and smiled. "Thanks, Gwen. I've never had a Bible. Where do I begin reading?"

"I like John's Gospel—where the ribbon marker is. Start there."

That evening before she went to sleep, Heather read the first chapter of John's Gospel. Some of it she understood, a lot she didn't. But her heart fixed on the phrase, "of his grace have we all received, even grace upon grace." As she repeated the phrase over and over, grace came over her and an unexplainable calm. She went to sleep peaceful, prepared for the next's day surgery.

Heather and her mother were put to sleep the following day in the same operating room in a Charleston hospital known as MUSC

(Medical University of South Carolina). Dr. Thomson had gotten the best kidney-transplant surgeons in the state to do the operation. Heather's worst kidney was removed, and one of her mother's kidneys was transplanted into her daughter. (Heather's other kidney, which only had 25% function, was not removed so as to help her through the recovery.) Her mother, who had given Heather life seventeen years before, was now giving her a second life. The two survived surgery well, and the transplant seemed to be a success. Time would tell if the new kidney would take to her body.

At first, it looked like everything was going to go well for Heather, but then her body reacted poorly to the new kidney. She started spiking fevers between 104 and 105 degrees. She got the shakes, and started to go delirious. Her fever kept spiking and spiking, indicating that her body was fighting an internal infection. What had happened was that the new kidney was absorbing fluids, medicines, antibiotics, but not filtering them. The medical staff knew they had to flush her system with as much fluid as possible in hopes of getting filtration through the kidney. They hooked her up to kidney dialysis immediately. If this didn't work, the doctors would have to remove the kidney and try again.

However, there were no other known matches. Heather's brother was not even close, and the same for her dad. Heather wouldn't die right away if they had to remove her newly transplanted kidney, but her days would be numbered. Her father knew this stark reality.

Dr. Thomson had never been a religious man, just a kind man and a reasonable one. He treated his patients with kindness and with reason. But this situation needed more than kindness and more than reason. And his daughter needed more than the best of modern medicine. She was struggling for her life. And he was agonizing as to how to give her life. There was only one solution, he figured; it had to come from beyond the human realm. It had to come from God. Dr. Thomson had a problem with this, however. He had never once in his life talked to God.

He left Heather's bedside, took her Bible, and went into the hospital chapel. He got down on his knees, wanted to say something, but no words came. He stared at the scene depicted in the stained-glass window in the upper archway of the chapel, a scene in which Jesus is laying his hands on a man kneeling before him. Then he opened the Bible to the page where the bookmarker was, the first chapter of John. He read the opening words:

"In the beginning was the Word, and the Word was with God, and the Word was God. He was in the beginning with God. All things came into being through him, and apart from him nothing came into being. Whatever was created was created by his life, and his life was the light of men."

Dr. Thomson was stunned by these words. He read them again and then again. Then it dawned on him, like that ray of sunlight piercing the stained-glass window in the chapel: all life and light come from God. He is the lifegiver and lightgiver. In one single flash, he saw it—Jesus laying hands on a man meant that Jesus was giving that man life. Not thinking of himself, Dr. Thomson cried out to God, "Oh give my daughter life!" And then he said, "I need your light."

He stayed there for a long time on his knees, soaking in the rays of God, until his spiritual revery was interrupted by his son tapping him on the shoulder. "Dad, good news. Heather's fever broke." From that moment on, Heather began to recover. Her mother's kidney took to her body and she had new life. The father brought his daughter and wife home from the hospital with a gladdened heart. Both would need time to recover, especially Heather.

Charlie was happy to have his best friend back again. He lay at the feet of her bed all day, biding his time by chewing on a bone or just napping. Since no one in the family had time to take him on beach walks, Gwen volunteered to do it after school.

The beach is empty in January. The only visible wildlife are seagulls and a few brave souls moving against the wind coming off the ocean. When a nor'eastern is kicking up, it's painful to walk against the wind. That's when Gwen would always remember the Irish blessing, "May the sun rise to greet you. May the wind always be at your back." She would laugh as she recited it, thinking how absurd it is to hope that the wind would always be at your back. "That would mean you never turned around," she said to the wind.

She threw a stick into the oncoming wind and watched it sail back over her head. Charlie got it and returned it to her feet. He didn't mind any kind of wind or any kind of cold. He was always glad to have the wide open spaces, the vast stretch of his layered universe: a long strip of sandy beach, next to a huge swath of flowing sea, over which spread the aqua skies. Gwen never tired of this scene, as well, which was always changing color and texture. She especially liked dusk, when the mauve hues of the dying sun cast a vermillion sheen on the shimmering sea. She stood there awed by God's good creation until twilight. Then she had to take Charlie home as the winter day turned suddenly dark.

Everyone had been so focused on Heather's health, even Heather herself, that no one really noticed that Charlie had lost a lot of weight. It had also escaped Gwen's notice. One morning in early February, while Heather was rubbing his stomach, she felt one of his ribs protruding, and then she felt another. "Oh, Charlie, you haven't been eatin' well. You got skinny like me. Gotta get you some steak." That night she talked to her parents about Charlie's eating. She insisted that he be fed real good meat. They agreed when they both took a good long look at him. Charlie was really getting thin.

Chapter Twenty-six

Bad News Again

As February ended and March began, springtime came to the seacoast of South Carolina. The dogwoods started to bloom, as did the Confederate jasmine. Soon the magnolia trees would burst open with puffs of bright white magnolia blossoms. The grass changed colors, from dead brown to verdant green; the air changed weight from thin frigidity to thick balminess. The turtles showed their heads again, the alligators slithered in the local ponds, and flocks of herons returned to feed.

Everywhere there were signs of spring, except in Charlie. His body got thinner. His brown eyes lost their luster. His runs on the beach got shorter. His naps longer. Heather and family knew there was something really wrong. The veterinarian, Dr. Carmichael, confirmed it when he gave them the results of some urine and blood tests: "I'm so sorry. Charlie is having kidney failure."

No one in the family could believe it. No one would believe it. No one could bring themselves to even think that Charlie had the same disease that Heather had had. No one would allow themselves to think that Charlie could die. They all lived in denial for over two weeks, refusing to accept the fact that their beloved Charlie could be dying of kidney failure. No one could absorb it, even Dr. Thomson who was medically trained. After all he had just gone through with his daughter and wife, he couldn't accept the fact that Charlie would die of kidney failure. They bought him special food. They gave him extra love. They hoped he would recover.

Heather took him on walks, talked to Charlie, and talked to God. "Jesus," she said, "if you could get me through kidney failure, you can get Charlie through it. There's gotta be a way." When she looked at Charlie, she just wanted to cry. But she checked herself, made herself strong, bent down beside him or kneeled beside him, and gave him long strong hugs. "Come on, Charlie, you can make it. You can do it. Come on, Lord, make him better. Pleeeeease—Lord, Oh, please."

Having realized that her life could have ended and that she was given second breath, she appreciated everything around her so very much. The blue sky was really blue. The green grass was made up of tiny leaves, each leaf alive. The world was full of intricately made insects, with different wings, antennae, color patterns, and shapes of legs. All creatures were alive by the same breath, the same sustaining spirit of God. She wanted that spirit, that life to sustain Charlie, to breathe into his being and keep him there forever—or, at least, as long as a dog should live. "It's not fair," she said to the Lord, "he's only four! Oh Lord, give him more years."

After that week, they took Charlie to Dr. Carmichael for more tests. The results were not encouraging. However, Dr. Carmichael told them that he had seen certain dogs live several years with kidney problems. With his Southern draw, he said, "Somehow some dogs just learn to cope with it. Let's hope the best for Charlie."

But during the next two weeks Charlie would hardly eat anything. His kidneys were rejecting any form of protein. He would take two bites of the special canine food and nothing more. Heather ate some in his presence to try to get him to eat more, but he wouldn't. The only thing he would eat was dog biscuits. Maybe two a day. Maybe one and a half. Fortunately, he drank a lot of water. Heather encouraged him to keep drinking and drinking. He did. But then he vomited his water and he vomited what little he had eaten. She ate dog biscuits in his presence, trying to get him to eat more. He'd eat maybe one bite, then go to the corner of the room and vomit.

One evening that week as the family was taking their evening meal, Heather burst into tears and said, "Charlie is dying. He's dying." They all burst into tears and cried uncontrollably. Reality had hit hard. As they were crying, Charlie walked into the kitchen. They all got down on the floor, circled around Charlie, laid their hands on him, and silently prayed. After this, Heather was so distraught that she left the house. She went to the backyard, clung to the trunk of a pine tree, and cried until she couldn't cry anymore. That whole night she clung to Charlie on her bed, crying and groaning, asking God to spare his life. "You spared my life. Spare Charlie's. Lord, you gotta love Charlie as much as me. I love him. Don't you?"

The next few days were dreadful. Charlie was emaciated. He wouldn't eat and hardly had any energy to walk. Heather could tell that he was really suffering. So could the whole family. When Dr. Thomson tried to talk to Heather about having Charlie put to sleep, she screamed, "No! Charlie is not leaving us!" Heather couldn't bear the thought of having Charlie euthanized. It deeply troubled her that humans had such power over animals. "Who are we that we can end the life of an animal?" she pondered. Distraught and filled with great anxiety, Heather could hardly sleep that night. She questioned God. She questioned life. She questioned everything. Nothing was right.

Gwen came over the next morning to try to bring some cheer into the bleak scene. As they sat on her back deck overlooking the pine woods, Heather asked her, "Does God love dogs?"

"Yea, sure. He loves everything he made."

"Then why does everything he makes die? What's the sense in that?"

"Don't really know, Heather. But I know God loves Charlie because you love Charlie. So let's pray for Charlie, okay?"

After the prayer, Gwen tried to distract Heather by encouraging her to go online with her, to explore the internet and things, since neither one of them had done this much. Heather reluctantly agreed. They looked up U.S. women's soccer events, surfing reports, and other things. When Gwen left, Heather stayed on line. She typed in the search box: "dog kidney failure." As she read all the various articles, she couldn't hold back her tears. Nothing sounded hopeful until she saw an article about a dog who received a kidney transplant. The University of California, Davis, School of Veterinary Medicine had performed a few successful kidney transplants in dogs.

After she read this, she sprang to her feet, ran to the backyard, where her parents were doing some gardening, and urged them to come in immediately. When they read the article, they agreed with Heather: "Charlie is going to have a transplant!" The first thing the next morning Dr. Thomson was on the phone with the specialists at the University of California. The head veterinarian was Dr. Cane. After listening to Dr. Thomson he told him, "We would be glad to do this for Charlie if—given his condition—you could bring him immediately. And you have to know—I must tell you up front—that the transplant will cost about $15,000. And you will have to pay out another $10,000 a year to give the dog high doses of immunosuppression drugs."

Dr. Thomson didn't hesitate for a second. "We'll have Charlie there as soon as possible and the money soon after."

"And there's one other thing," Dr. Cane added. "Charlie needs a near perfect match. Does he have any brothers or sisters? One of them could donate a kidney and still live fine."

"We don't know where his litter mates are. But we do know where his son is."

"That will be good enough. You need to secure permission from the owner to do this. I'll fax the paperwork."

As Mrs. Thomson was making the flight arrangements, Dr. Thomson went down their street to ask Mr. Plymouth if he would allow Spin, Charlie's one-year-old son, to donate one of his kidneys. Mr. Plymouth was stunned by this request and flatly refused. His daughter overheard the conversation, walked into the living room, and said, "But, Daddy—wouldn't we want someone to do this for us if Spin was gonna die? Spin's his only chance."

"Please," Dr. Thomson urged. "Here is the number of Dr. Cane in California. He will assure you that Spin can live with one kidney. My daughter, Heather, is living just fine with one kidney. And so is my wife. I will pay you well for this."

"How much?" Mr. Plymouth queried.

"I'll give you $5,000."

Mr. Plymouth hesitated, looked down at his daughter's plaintive face and said, "Okay, it's a deal."

The plans were then made for Heather to go to California with Charlie and Spin. Dr. and Mrs. Thomson had missed way too many days of work already. They could not afford to take any more days off, especially since they had a bill of $15,000 to pay, and another $5,000 to Mr. Plymouth.

Since both of Charlie's kidneys had failed, this was a make-or-break surgery. He would either die shortly after surgery or come out with a new life. The Thomsons were aware of the realities. Heather, gripped with fear, trying to show courage, stayed with Charlie the first day in the clinic, where he got infusions of nutrients and a round of antibiotics before he went into surgery.

She stayed in the clinic all night, as well, sleeping on a sofa in the waiting room. Every hour or so, she walked into his room, and stroked him all over—his stomach, his back, his head, his legs. He was skin and bones, a ghost of his former self. She refused to cry. She told him, "Charlie. Tomorrow, you will sleep and dream. Then when you get up, you will be good. We will run the beach again, you and me. We will swim. We will surf. We will chase pelicans. We will run after the sun." Then she pet Spin and told him, "You are my hero, boy. You are the best."

In the morning, they took Charlie and Spin off to surgery. The scene reminded her poignantly of the one where she and her mother were being rolled in together to the operating room in MUSC. Heather paced the waiting room in the clinic, went outside for fresh air, prayed, read her Bible, watched the clock, called her parents on the phone every half-hour or so, paced some more, watched the clock, went outside for more air, and went from hope to despair to hope every other minute. Late that afternoon, one of the doctors came into the waiting room, looking quite serious. Then he smiled when he realized what his demeanor did to Heather's countenance. He told her, "The transplant is done. Both dogs are in recovery now. Both of them should do fine with one kidney."

"I know," Heather answered, "I'm the same. I've got one good kidney transplanted from my mother."

"Lucky you!" He smiled. "We've stabilized Charlie. He's got good breathing going now. We've got antibiotics and nutrients pumping into him, as well as immunosuppressives. He should make it if his body takes the new kidney. You just keep praying. We believe in that 'round here. Spin is doing just fine. He's a very healthy retriever."

Heather immediately called her parents with the news. Dr. Thomson started to explain to Heather everything that would happen in the next 24 hours—that is, medically speaking. Heather said, "I know, Dad, I've been through this myself. I know what Charlie is going to go through. Let's all pray that the good kidney takes."

Chapter Twenty-seven

Homecoming

Charlie recovered slowly but surely, to the joy of everyone on the medical staff, to the extreme elation of Heather, to the relief and joy of Dr. and Mrs. Thomson, as well to many people back home in Pawleys Island who had been praying for Charlie and Spin and cheering for them. On the third day after his surgery, Charlie was well enough to recognize Heather when she came to his side. He wagged his tail when she came near, flapping it on the bed like a drumstick. What a joyous sound, better than all the music she had ever heard. Charlie was alive and fairly well. Spin was as good as ever. He was up and about within a few days.

After two more weeks of convalescing, Charlie was ready to go home. Mrs. Thomson flew out to California and rented a car for the drive back to South Carolina. They thought it would be too traumatic for Charlie to be put in a cage and in cargo. The medical staff gave Charlie and Spin a cheery bon voyage. Charlie, their fifth successful kidney-transplant, had become dear to all of them. And they were all so proud of Spin. Charlie had started to gain weight. The luster in his coat was returning, as well as the glow in his eyes. They would miss Charlie and Spin.

On their return to South Carolina, Charlie and Spin were welcomed by Dr. Thomson, the Plymouths, all of Heather's soccer team, many neighbors, and many members of the community. They gave Charlie dog treats galore, most of which would not be part of his special diet. And the community gave the Thomsons a collective gift of $6,500. Overwhelmed, the Thomsons thanked them all for their graciousness and thoughtfulness.

The doctors told Heather that Charlie would need special care, especially with regard to diet and exercise. They wrote out the entire regimen. Dr. Carmichael, apprised of the whole situation, would follow up on all Charlie's care. He needed special food, vitamins, pure drinking water, and high doses of immunosuppression drugs. And he needed to avoid extreme temperature changes. So they strictly forbade any swimming in the ocean when the water was under 72 degrees. This meant that Charlie could swim only in June, July, August, and early September. And they made it clear that he could swim only for short periods.

Since Heather's regimen was the nearly same for maintaining her health, she found it no problem whatsoever to be vigilant for Charlie. The rest of that spring and summer Heather had two focuses and only two—the recovery of her health and Charlie's. Well—she also had a lot of schooling to make up, if she was going to be permitted to start in the autumn as a senior. Both she and Charlie walked together, slowly ran together, and chased the sun together—just as she had promised him before his surgery. And when she studied, he sat beside her or slept beside her. When mid-June came, they even swam together. Gwen joined Heather for a few surf sessions when the waves were clean and easy to take. From that day on, Charlie always watched them surf. He never again wanted to get on the board, and Heather never asked him to.

He had too much fun on shore. All the locals knew him, and wanted to come up to him and pet him. This attention and touching meant that Charlie had to get a sterilizing bath every evening, as well as take an antibacterial mouthwash. He didn't mind the bath, but he hated the mouthwash. As a reward for taking it, he would get a special treat. Then he had to be thoroughly dried and stay in his climate-controlled house, about 72 degrees. Of course, Heather knew that this meant his outside activities during winter would be cut off, so she wanted to make the most of summer.

They continued their early morning sessions on the beach because this was their special time and because there were less humans and other dogs around. If the waves were good, Heather would surf, but only for 20 to 30 minutes, so as not to exhaust herself. Charlie would wade in the shallows and occasionally swim but only for a few minutes. He intuitively knew his limits. He had given up chasing birds and, instead, tried to catch the minnows that race back to sea after a wave has crashed on shore and spread out into a thin layer of water. He could see all these little fish sprinting back to deeper waters, streaming past his ankles, and he wanted to get one.

If it was raining in the morning, Heather would often take Charlie to the beach the last hour of the day before sunset instead of in the morning. This happened one particular August day, when it rained all morning, then cleared up by late afternoon. When she took Charlie to the beach, she saw that the waves were gorgeous—about chest high and glassy, blown by a southwestern wind. She joined a few surfers on the north side of the pier, who enjoyed an hour of pure fun waves. As the hour passed by, the group had drifted farther and farther north with the current. As always, Charlie followed Heather's every move, staying parallel with her on the beach. Then the winds shifted and started blowing harder directly from the south.

One by one the other surfers got out of the water as dusk was turning to twilight. Heather, alone in the water, started to panic when she realized that she had drifted to the north inlet. She tried to turn her board toward the northern tip of the island, but the current was far too strong. She thought, *If I could catch a wave, it might take me to the other side of the inlet.* She saw a big wave coming, paddled for it, went to her feet, slipped, and badly wiped out. As she fell, her board flipped up and came crashing down on her head, cutting her forehead.

Still leashed to her board, she managed to pull the board back to her and get on it. Charlie had followed her all the way to the end of the island. When he saw that she was drifting to the other side of the inlet, he jumped into the sea to swim to her. Both of them were caught in a very strong current that swept them into the inlet instead of beyond it. Heather lay on her board and went with the flow. There was nothing else she could do. But then—in the last light of dusk—she saw Charlie desperately swimming across the inlet to get to her. His head rose just above the waves, as he took each wave in turn, flailing with his front paws to get over the top of each break. She turned her board toward him and paddled with all her strength against the flow. Though she wasn't getting anywhere, at least she wasn't allowing herself to go with the current. And this gave Charlie the chance to catch up with her. As he neared, she hollered, "Charlie! Charlie! Com' on, boy!"

When he was five feet from her, she reached out her arms and called to him again. As he neared, she grabbed him and lifted up on the surfboard, while she slid off the board and positioned herself behind it. From there, she could steer the board and keep Charlie afloat. The current took them straight into the inlet and creek that encircles the island. Exhausted, she had no other choice but to go with the flow. By now, there was no more trace of sunset. Darkness had dropped on earth. As they drifted down the creek to the south, they slid through the marsh on their right and beach houses on their left.

Heather eventually got her sense of location. She knew where there was a boat landing on this side of the island, not far from where she had parked her car, but she wasn't sure she had the strength to get the board over there. As she neared the landing, which was lit by a couple of light posts, she saw a couple of fishermen who were just about to pull their boat out of the water with their pickup truck. She shouted out, "Help! Can you catch us? Help!"

The driver heard the call, quickly got out of his truck, and waded out into the water. His buddy did the same. They had to stand their ground against a swift current and make their way out to Heather and Charlie. One of them fell on the slippery boat ramp that runs underneath the water, but the other managed to make it to Heather and Charlie. He held out his hand until Heather caught hold. Charlie got off the board and swam to shore. The two men then helped Heather get to shore, as she dragged her surfboard behind her.

"Dang, girl. What ya doin' surfin' in the creek? That's plum crazy!" one of them said, while the other quickly added, "And takin' your dog?" The two went on and on about how crazy it was for Heather to be surfing the creek—and with a dog.

Under the lights, Heather could see that these guys were good ol' boys. The Confederate flag on the back windshield just beneath the shotgun rack was a telltale sign, as well as the way they wore their long hair in ponytails, swore, and spit tobacco juice after each sentence.

Then one of them said, "That's a nice retriever ya got there. Does he hunt?"

"No," Heather remarked, as she wiped away the blood from her forehead.

"See ya got cut there, girl. Need a lift somewhere?"

"No thanks."

"Ah com' on. Ya'll can jus' jump in the back."

"No thanks."

Then one of them approached Charlie, as he was shaking himself dry. Charlie backed off as the man got closer. When the man held out his hand, Charlie showed his teeth and snarled. "What's with him?" he retorted, as he withdrew his hand.

"Long story," Heather replied softly.

When the pickup drove away, Heather and Charlie walked side by side down the island road under a moonlit sky. Heather could tell that Charlie was cold but not shivering. She cursed herself for being so stupid and asked the Lord for his forgiveness. When they reached her car, she put away her surfboard, got down on her knees next to Charlie, and gave him a long strong hug.

Afterword

This story of Charlie was based, in part, on the real life story of my dog, Charlie, a golden retriever. This is the tribute I wrote for him in the local newspaper (Pawleys Island, South Carolina) after he died of kidney failure and went on to the next life:

A Tribute to Charlie

Several years ago my wife and I were talking about how sad we would be when our Shetland sheep dog, Barnie, would have to die. Our youngest son, Peter, was about five then. He overheard our conversation and completely took us by surprise when he said, "Don't worry, Mom and Dad, Barnie will be a dog angel!"

Barnie passed on, as did another dog dear to us, named Nanook, a Siberian husky. Then another dog came into our lives in a most unexpected way. My wife, Georgia, was on her way down highway 17 to Charleston to find housing for our youngest son, Peter, for his freshman year at College of Charleston. There's a long stretch of pine woods known as Francis Marion Reserve, running south of McClellanville to just north of Charleston. On the way, she saw what she thought was a young deer emerging from the woods onto the brim of the highway. Having passed several logging trucks on the way, she feared for the deer's life. She quickly turned around and went back to help him. When she got closer, she saw it was a dog.

Opening the front door, she said, "Come on. Get in." And he did. Emaciated, dirt-covered, and full of ticks, he looked over at Georgia with those deep brown eyes overflowing with thankfulness. She took him to the nearest vet in Mt. Pleasant, who agreed to clean him up, take away all the ticks, and check out his health. When she returned to get him, she couldn't believe what she saw: a beautiful golden retriever, whom she immediately named Charleston. The vet told her he must have survived the woods for three to four weeks. He had wild boar marks on his belly, showing he had been through some battles. He was dehydrated, exhausted, barely alive.

Charleston came home with us, grateful for everything. During the first week, he regained his strength, soaking in all the love he could get. When he approached me, he would sit before me, and hold his right paw out for me to shake. Then he would lay down to sleep. He warmed me with his gentle presence, ever more and more as spring grew into summer.

Soon Charleston started going with me to the beach. I don't think he had ever been to the ocean in the year and half of his life. The first trip there he chased all the sandpipers, then the seagulls, and then pelicans. He loved to wade out with me, and swim around as I surfed. Eventually, he enjoyed getting on the surfboard, and riding a wave or two all the way in to shore. Anyone who saw him ride in a wave would wave and cheer. I'll never forget one wave, where Charlie rode it on all the way—from fifty yards out to the shallow waters. He just stepped off the board from water to land, pranced through a group of cheering onlookers and on down the shore to the next adventure. Charlie (for that is what we started calling him) made everyone smile. His soul was radiant.

He loved the beach of Pawleys Island where he could run and run, swim and swim, chase the migrating swarms of bluefish, follow the flow of leaping dolphins, and dally with sand crabs. And Charlie loved to mingle with the surfers, as they went down the shore, into and out of the water. I never had to worry about him running off. No matter where I was in the water and he was on shore, he would keep an eye on me, and follow me if I drifted in the current. Every time I caught a wave, he would run parallel to me and meet me in the shallows. He was as excited as I was that I had rode a wave. Charlie showed it by prancing up to me in the shallows, wagging his tail, beaming with pure joy.

Everyone loved Charlie at the beach. He was a good soul, a free spirit, a kind expression of a gentle Creator still creating and sustaining his universe. He helped us see the small wonders of nature. He made us laugh, and enjoy what is—not what should have been or what will be. To be with Charlie was to be.

And so it came to us like some hellish nightmare when we discovered that he had major kidney failure—incurable and mortal. As his body wasted away, we tried to keep him alive on love and water. We stroked his stomach again and again—his favorite—and told him, "We love you, Charlie." After a few weeks, there was no flesh on his ribs. To stroke his body was to touch his bones—and to touch his soul which didn't want to go.

It was so hard to say goodbye to our other dogs—to Barney and to Nanook. But they lived full and fulfilling lives. But Charlie had graced this earth for only four years, and now he had to go, and there was nothing we could do. So we gave his soul to God and his spirit to the wind that moves the waves and warms the earth.

When I brought him to the vet on that final day, the vet took him from my arms and said, "Come on, angel."

A Poem for Charlie

the beach is his. he makes it. the darting minnows
in surge, suck, sally. the sandpipers scurrying
between swooshes. the dallies with clawing crabs.
the pelicans bobbing on the sea like sun.
the swim, the search in crushed waves for the stick I pitched.
the fetch, prance, strut—like a majorette, he waves the stick
as high in the air as he can get it.
he is good so good. it is his universe.
those who stroll by sense, catch, smile, and share the glow
as we kick our way through the shallows
northward headed—I with board in hand and he with stick in jaw—
and slosh our way to the northern tip
where I begin to surf nor'eastern wind waves and slide wind down
southbound breaking lefts, all the while trailed
by my companion who watches my catches and follows my drift
excited by every ride, he runs along, my terrestrial shadow.
and even if I mingle with a swarm of other black garbed surfers
he stays fixed on me until I ride the last wave to shore
where I am met in the shallows by the sweetest soul
with dance, swagger, primal joy, contagious happiness—
he wants more. so much more. never to leave the surging sea—
to chase dogs, rays, and falcons, to fetch, catch anything called life
but I exhausted soaked and spent, coax him toward the exit,
where we pass many a local who don't known my name
nor I theirs, but they call out anyway: "Charlie! How's the surf?"

Printed in the United States
42556LVS00002B/40-87

9 781413 765366